A Mermaid in Middle Grade

in

Middle Grade

BOOK 1
THE TALISMAN OF LOSTLAND

KNOWLEDGE FOREST
PRESS

A.M. LUZZADER

Published by Knowledge Forest Press
P.O. Box 6331
Logan, UT 84341

Paperback ISBN-13: 978-1-949078-10-7
Hardback ISBN-13: 978-1-949078-12-1
Ebook ISBN-13: 978-1-949078-11-4

Cover design by Sleepy Fox Studio
Developmental and Copy Editing by Chadd VanZanten and
Barbra Yardley
Proofreading by Telltail Editing (telltailediting.com)
Interior illustrations by Chadd VanZanten

For my mother, Barbra
Thank you for encouraging creativity and imagination

*T*here were many occupations and jobs under the sea that young mermaids and mermen might have when they grew up. They could become teachers, police officers, or dentists. Some merfolk grew up to design homes and office buildings; others built them. There were merfolk doctors and artists and scientists. Merfolk chose the occupation that best suited their interests and talents. But there was one responsibility that belonged to all merfolk.

Magic.

The merfolk were the guardians of the ocean, the protectors of the sea, and they used mer-magic to keep the sea life safe and healthy. It was a responsibility that all merpeople took very seriously.

Brynn Finley had been told about mer-magic and guarding the sea from the time she was a wee merbaby. When she was just five years old, Brynn asked her parents, "When I grow up, I'll be a guardian of the sea, too? Like you?"

"That's right," her mom, Dana, answered. "You'll be a guardian of the sea."

"How can I guard the whole sea?" Brynn asked, looking around at what seemed like an endless aquamarine ocean.

Brynn's father chuckled. His name was Adrian. "You won't be the only guardian," he said, "and you don't have to guard the whole sea by yourself. You'll help your mom and me at first. Then, I have a feeling we'll end up helping you."

Brynn's dad was not a big or powerful merman. He didn't have the bulging muscles or the long golden hair that many other mermen had. Adrian wasn't a mighty mer-warrior or intrepid undersea explorer—he worked in a restaurant and was an excellent chef. He was sort of skinny, too, didn't even have a beard. His blue hair was short, and he wore eyeglasses. However, behind the glasses, Adrian's eyes were kind, and Brynn knew he was one of the smartest mermen around.

"We all help out with the guardian thing," Adrian told Brynn. "We each do our part."

But the ocean is so huge, Brynn thought. She furrowed her brow and blinked her deep blue eyes.

Adrian tousled Brynn's flowing lavender hair.

"Don't worry about it too much," added Adrian. "When you start learning mer-magic, you'll get it."

Brynn was now twelve years old and almost ready for middle school. She wasn't very tall, but her hair was even longer now, and her tailfin was a dazzling shade of teal. She was also beginning to understand what a noble and important responsibility it was to take care of life in the ocean. She watched her mom and dad work on undersea problems, and it made her proud to be a mermaid.

And so, when a little pod of dolphins came to the underwater cave that the Finley family called home, Brynn paid close attention. Brynn's father invited the dolphins inside. They clicked and whistled urgently at him. Brynn stayed in the hallway, but floated forward to listen. The dolphins whistled and squeaked.

Brynn didn't understand any of it.

Now, it's not easy to understand and speak to dolphins, and in fact, Brynn wasn't even sure how to say "hello" or "where's the bathroom?" in dolphin-speak. No one did. But her father folded his slender arms and nodded as the dolphins chattered away. Like most merfolk, he was able to communicate with them using mer-magic.

Not many species of sea creatures could express themselves clearly enough to communicate. Nautiluses might be very pretty, for example, with their dramatically striped, spiraling shell and their striking eyes, but they didn't have much to say. Same with jellyfish and sea cucumbers—kind of boring, to tell the truth. It was impossible to get anything at all out of a sea sponge.

Octopuses, on the other hand, were very well spoken, and were well known for their humor. But many other fish and sea creatures simply did not have much to say beyond a few simple moods and feelings. In fact, lots of fish seemed to have only two settings: "hungry" and "sleepy," and they repeated these words constantly depending on how they were feeling. The slightly more complex sea animals might also be able to communicate fear or danger.

As most people know, dolphins are highly intelligent. It was said that they were as intelligent as merfolk in some ways, and so many ages ago, the merpeople and dolphins had learned to work together. The dolphins were the eyes and ears of the ocean. They alerted merpeople to problems and emergencies, and the merpeople used their mer-magical powers to help.

And this is why Brynn knew, even without understanding what the dolphins were saying, that there was trouble somewhere in the sea close by. At first, she listened from her bedroom, but then she swam out into the hallway. Her father spotted her. He turned his head and gave her a quick, friendly wink. Then he turned his attention to the dolphins again, using his mer-magic to respond and ask questions. The dolphins gestured with their fins and noses as though pointing and giving directions. Adrian nodded.

Brynn knew that whatever the emergency was, her father would go to help. She knew this because her parents always helped when the dolphins came. It usually happened the same way—the dolphins arrived, her father or mother used mer-magic to speak with them, and then they would announce they had to go.

"We've got a lost baby humpback whale," Brynn's mom might say. "There's a search party. Back before dinner—hopefully!"

A few nights later, it might be her dad who took the call. "The lady octopus up the reef got into some toxic sludge—I'll go see what I can do."

There was always excitement in the water when the calls came in—even when the trouble was dire. And sometimes there was nothing they could do—like the time that giant ocean liner hit that nice old sunfish. However, no matter what the situation, Brynn's parents were always eager, determined, and ready to do what they could to help. And although Brynn had not yet been allowed to join them, she knew they were heroes, and that they were fulfilling the merfolk oath.

But this night was different.

As the dolphins swam away, Adrian turned to his daughter, his face thoughtful.

"What's up, Dad?" Brynn asked, drifting into the front room. "Is it serious?"

"A young sea turtle's in trouble," he said.

"You gonna go and help?"

"Yeah," he replied. "He's nearby. I'll go and see what can be done."

Brynn nodded, wondering what the problem was. Was it injured? Trapped somehow? Sick? How did her father always know what to do?

Adrian turned, and from a nook in the cavern wall, he retrieved a knife in a sheath strung on a chain. He always took the knife on missions. Brynn's mother had one, too. Adrian looped the chain around his neck and drifted toward the front door, but then he paused and turned to Brynn again.

"Hey, Brynn," he said, almost casually, "how'd you like to come along?"

Brynn's eyes widened. "Who, *me*? Come with *you*?" She pointed at the door. "To—to go and save a turtle?"

"Yeah," her dad replied. "You're gonna be learning all about this stuff in middle school this year. You'll be talking to dolphins and doing mer-magic on your own, real soon. I think it's time you came along on a mission."

Brynn almost didn't know how to answer. Of course, she knew that she would help out eventually. Her parents, teachers, neighbors, relatives—they all told her she'd be a guardian of the sea on some faraway day.

But, apparently, that day was today.

At first, Brynn was practically paralyzed with excitement.

"Okay," cried Brynn at last. "Yeah, sure! Wowee!" She darted around the front room of the cavern. "What should I bring? My backpack? A notebook? Toothbrush? Snacks?"

Brynn's dad laughed and put a hand on her shoulder. "Nah. Just go tell your mom you're coming with me. But hurry. We don't want him to wait too long. We have to go fast."

A few minutes later, as Brynn's mother stood waving from the front door of their cave, Brynn and her dad set out to see about the sea turtle.

"Hold onto my neck, Brynn," said her father.

Brynn wondered if she was perhaps too old to ride on her dad's back, but none of her classmates were around to see, and she wouldn't start middle school until next week, so she decided it would be okay. The truth was, she loved holding onto her dad's neck while he swam. For a skinny guy, he was a really strong swimmer. His mer-magic allowed him to soar rapidly through the ocean. It was like holding onto a barracuda chasing a skipjack. The water rushed past, and Brynn's long lavender hair swirled furiously behind them.

Sometimes, when Brynn was around her classmates, she wished that her father looked more like those other mermen—the ones with the muscles and heavy scales and mossy beards. But as she held onto his neck as he coursed smoothly and speedily toward her very first sea mission, Brynn knew her dad really was powerful. He was a good merman, his mer-magic was strong, and he cared about others. Her mother, too, was smart and kind.

And now that Brynn was going to middle school, she would learn mer-magic, too, and begin her duty as a sea guardian.

Adrian sailed through a shoal of sardines, and the shiny fish scattered in a silvery sunburst. Brynn laughed as they darted through her hair. But she felt nervous, too.

At last, her father slowed, and Brynn let go of his neck and swam beside him. The dolphins had directed them to the shallows along an island, where sunlight sparkled on the sea's surface and shone in the water in warm, golden rays. They swam over the reef, where coral sprouted for miles in shades of pink and orange and blue. The coral reef was always lively, with lots of fish, crabs, shrimp, sharks, and other sea life.

"See a turtle anywhere?" asked Adrian.

"No," said Brynn.

To their right were some wildly patterned parrot-fish, pecking at the coral with their sharp beaks. A school of stately groupers floated slowly by, their giant gills flaring. The nervous little sardines and tropical fish swarmed everywhere.

Then Brynn spotted a little sea turtle over in a clump of coral. He struggled weakly against something unseen that seemed to hold him in place.

"Dad," she cried. "Over there! Is that him?"

Adrian looked. "That's gotta be him! Good eye, kiddo!"

"What's the matter with him?" she asked as they swam closer.

"Tangled in fishing line," said Adrian. "I kinda thought that might be the problem."

The sea turtle was snagged up on the reef by shreds of an old fishing net made of ghostly filaments of pale, greenish blue. The turtle's legs and even his head were wound and wrapped in the almost unbreakable line.

"This happens a lot," said Adrian as they drew close to the turtle. "He tried to free himself, but that usually only makes things worse."

Sea turtles are clad in a tough, leathery hide, but Brynn saw that the net had tightened so fiercely that it was cutting into the young turtle's flesh. The turtle thrashed and flopped but couldn't get free, and it probably needed to surface for air. In Brynn's opinion, sea turtles wore a rather glum expression under the best of circumstances, with their big sad eyes, but this one looked sad and terrified and miserable all at the same time.

Adrian unsheathed the knife around his neck. It was made from a shard of a giant clamshell and was savagely sharp.

"Brynn?" said her dad. "See if you can calm the little fella down while I cut some of this line."

Brynn's heart was thumping like mad. Sea turtles weren't known to be particularly dangerous, but this was, technically, a wild sea animal, so Brynn didn't know what to expect. She reached out. The turtle flailed suddenly in panic. Brynn and her father drew back, then approached more slowly. Brynn again put her hand out and placed it on the turtle's shell. His eyes rolled with fear, and he watched Brynn suspiciously.

"It's okay," Brynn whispered. "We're here to help you."

"What a mess," said Adrian, cutting away a few strands of the net. He was trying to avoid cutting the turtle, but the miserable creature kept flapping its flippers, trying to swim free.

"Try to hold still, little guy," Brynn cooed. She ran her hand along his neck and shell. "Shh. It's gonna be okay."

The turtle didn't exactly understand the words Brynn was saying, but he seemed to catch her meaning. He held still for a few moments. Brynn patted him lightly on the shell.

"That's the way, Brynn," said Adrian, slicing

away more and more of the net as the turtle stopped moving so much. "Yeah, there we go."

"Good boy," Brynn whispered to the little turtle. "Hold still."

"Just this last bunch here," said Adrian, sawing away at the line with his knife, "and—there!"

Suddenly free, the turtle swam quickly away, but then he evidently ran out of energy, and he began to sink to the seafloor.

"Poor critter's exhausted and probably starved for air," said Adrian.

They swam over to the turtle and helped him swim toward the surface. Once they broke through the water, the turtle took a few gulps of air. In the bright sunshine, Brynn and her dad could clearly see the tiny red slices on the turtle's flippers and neck where the net had dug into him.

"Look, he's hurt!" said Brynn.

"Yeah," said Adrian. "That's common. Nets and fishing lines are so strong. It's very hard on sea creatures. But it's all right. I think I can heal him."

Adrian held his hands together as if cupping a ball. Then he closed his eyes. A sphere of white light appeared between his hands. When he opened his eyes, the sphere drifted toward the turtle. Then it expanded, growing larger until it engulfed the creature. Brynn watched in amazement as the cuts closed and nearly vanished. The young turtle's eyes narrowed with a kind of sleepy relief. Brynn had seen acts of mer-magic before, but not so close-up, and never on a mission to save a sea creature in the wild. Never like this.

The white magical energy dimmed, dispersed, and then disappeared.

"Mer-magical," Brynn whispered.

After that, the turtle seemed happy and quite at ease. Brynn laughed, and she and Adrian swam along with the young turtle for a while to make sure he was really okay.

"How does it work, Dad? How do you do spells like that?"

"Well," said Adrian, "that's what you're going to be learning in middle school. But I'll let you in on the big secret: basically, it consists of concentrating and directing your feelings of love for others toward the person or animal you're trying to heal. All mer-magic comes from love. That's the most important part to remember."

"That's it? That's all you do?"

"Well, I might be simplifying it just a little."

"It sounds easy!" cried Brynn.

Adrian laughed and shook his head. "For you? I have a feeling it will be."

Brynn thought it was the most wonderful thing she had ever seen. She pantomimed the motions she'd seen her dad making, conjuring the healing sphere. She couldn't wait to learn how to do it for real, even if that meant she had to go to school and learn the other, less-exciting subjects like social studies and math.

The sun was setting behind the little island and the young turtle seemed to be recovering perfectly.

"Well, we better get home," said Adrian. "Your mom will have dinner ready."

Brynn wrapped her arms around her dad's neck, but as they turned for home, Brynn noticed the turtle.

"Look, Dad! He's following us," said Brynn.

"Hm. Seems like you might have a pet," said Adrian, laughing.

Brynn hoped that was true.

They swam home by a different route, through a shallow sea canyon where there once was a valley of seagrass and moss but was now a field of garbage from the surface world. There were long lengths of fishing line, plastic food packaging, and debris that Brynn didn't even know the words for. There were merfolk in the valley, gathering the trash into massive bunches and bundles. Adrian slowed to check it out.

"Hop off, Brynn," he said with a sigh. "Let's help out a little."

The young turtle swam up from behind them and gloomily surveyed the scene.

"This is probably where our little pal picked up that fishing line," said Adrian.

It was an ongoing problem. The merfolk had been seeing more and more garbage in their areas of the ocean. Brynn and Adrian began hauling the garbage together, bundling it up with strands of the rope and fishing line.

"Where does it all come from?" Brynn asked. She scrunched her nose as she distastefully gathered in a swarm of dirty plastic packages, ruptured bottles, and seemingly endless drifts of shredded plastic sacks.

Adrian looked at his daughter sadly. "The humans who live on the land," he said.

"But why?" Brynn asked. "Why do they just throw their junk into our world?" She couldn't imagine throwing garbage into someone else's home.

"We're not really sure," said Adrian. "I suspect they just don't realize it's happening, like maybe they're just careless. Here, hold this pile steady while I wrap this fishing line around it."

Brynn wrinkled her nose again. She didn't like touching any of the trash. It felt dirty and gross, but she realized this was better than leaving it in the water and risking an animal eating it or getting trapped in it. The little sea turtle seemed to realize what they were doing and helped them push the garbage together as best he could. And so they worked until it was dark. Soon, much of the garbage was collected into great bundles. The other mer-workers began to haul the big bundles away. They waved at Brynn and her dad.

"Thank you for the hand!" they hollered.

Adrian waved back at them.

"Where will they take it all?" Brynn asked.

"The city council has designated some areas to hold it for now," he said as they continued on their way home. "But if this keeps up, we'll run out of room. There." Adrian pointed. "Look over there."

In the distance, Brynn saw one of the garbage holding areas, where huge piles of waste and debris were contained with nets woven from undersea moss. From a distance, they looked like underwater hills, but Brynn knew it was just tons of disgusting surface garbage.

"All of this is from the land-dwellers?" she asked. "It's gross."

Adrian nodded sadly but pressed forward in the water and propelled them the rest of the way home. When they reached their sea cave, the turtle was still with them.

"So, can I keep him?" Brynn asked.

"Sure, he's welcome to hang around the house for as long as he wants to," said her dad. "Just remember that they have to go up to the surface to get air every six hours or so."

"Don't worry," said Brynn "I'll walk him every day!"

"I guess you better give him a name, then," quipped Adrian.

Brynn looked at the turtle. "How about—Tully," she said.

The turtle swam happily around her, and then rubbed his nose on her face.

"I think he likes it," said Adrian.

"Tully the Turtle," said Brynn, patting Tully on his head.

That night, Adrian tucked Brynn into bed. Tully curled up by Brynn's tailfin. Adrian pulled a blanket over Brynn and kissed her on top of the head.

"Good job today, kiddo," said Adrian.

"It was so fun! Thanks for taking me along," said Brynn, happy but exhausted.

Adrian smiled. "Sure," he said. "You're not my little merbaby anymore, are ya? You're growing up."

Mer-homes were lit by rocks infused with mer-magic, which made them glow softly. As Adrian left Brynn's bedroom, he waved at the magic rocks and they went dark.

As Brynn snuggled into her watery bed, she heard the muffled voices of her parents talking in the kitchen. Brynn floated up out of bed and drifted over to the door.

"How was it?" asked Brynn's mother, Dana. "How'd she do?"

"Oh, she was great," replied Adrian. "That silly little turtle was all wrapped up in an old fishing net from the surface. And you know how it is with old fishing gear. You're trying to cut them free with this razor-sharp work knife and they're thrashing around and you come home with your fingers all cut up. But

Brynn jumped right in and got the turtle settled down, and we had him cut free in no time. It's gonna be nice to have a little helper."

"She's growing up fast," Dana admitted.

"Mm hm," said Adrian. "Someday she'll be a grown-up mermaid and then she'll swim away for good. No more dad-daughter fishing trips. No more sea rides. Where's the time gone?"

"Oh, don't be glum, hon," said Dana with a chuckle. "It's not like she's in there packing for college. And I'll bet you twenty sand dollars that she'll still be up for a sea ride even after she moves out."

Adrian laughed and said, "You're probably right."

"So, she really was helpful? She did a good job?"

"Oh, yeah," said Adrian, his voice pleased and excited again. "She's kind of a natural."

Brynn grinned and swam back to bed in a daze. A natural!

CHAPTER TWO

One night a few weeks later, with Tully dozing at the foot of her bed, Brynn had a marvelous dream. She dreamed that she'd learned all the mer-magical abilities, all the famous spells—protection and healing and hiding. Spells to swim fast and talk to animals and make plants grow.

Brynn dreamed she was taking care of all the animals of the sea—whales, sharks, whale sharks. She worked with the gentlest sea life, such as seahorses and jellyfish, but she helped those that were a little scary, too, like the great white sharks and the giant squid that dwelled down in the blackest depths of the sea. And in Brynn's dream, all the sea creatures were healthy and happy because of her magic, and in her dream, they were all her great friends—she could even speak to the sea sponges! Brynn dreamed that spells glowed and flowed from her fingertips in bright shades of purple and gold and brilliant white. In the dream, she was the most powerful and beloved mermaid there had ever been.

"You're the best sea guardian ever!" shouted the dolphins.

"You make the sea better wherever you go!" cried the sea lions.

"Thank you, Brynn!" thundered the whales.

But somewhere beneath all the adoration, there was another voice, and this one sounded annoyed. And also, someone was nudging or poking at her. In her dream, Brynn waved to the whales and bowed to the bluefin tunas and shook hands with the big puffy-headed wrasses, but that other voice grew more insistent.

"Brynn Finley! For the tenth time, wake up! You'll be late!"

Brynn opened her eyes and sat up in bed. She blinked groggily.

"Get up, Brynn, you silly fish!" It was Brynn's mother, Dana. She floated next to Brynn's bed, laughing but obviously a bit impatient. "Do you want to be late for your first day of middle school?"

Brynn yawned, stretched, and looked out the window. It was still dark outside. "School already? But it's so early."

"Yeah, but you still have to eat breakfast, get dressed, and take Tully for a walk to the surface. Now come on!"

Brynn's mother, Dana, was a very intelligent mermaid who had long, lovely, rose-colored hair. She was a researcher at the university, and her mer-magic was said to be second to none. She tweaked Brynn on the nose and, with a wave of her tail, swam out of the bedroom and into the kitchen.

When Brynn's mom was gone, Tully floated up, nuzzling Brynn for a pat on his head.

"Tully!" said Brynn, patting Tully on his broad, flat head and scratching his wrinkly neck. "I had the most amazing dream. I can't wait to do magic."

Brynn really was looking forward to school, but there were many things she was worried about, too. There'd be a lot more students than there'd been at her little elementary school. Brynn worried about fitting in, and she hoped she'd have classes with her best friend, Jade. Would the classes be hard? Would they be hard to find? Would she get lost between every period? And the teachers—would they be friendly or strict? And then there was the whole issue of recess—there wasn't any playtime in middle school, and Brynn knew for sure she would miss playing four-square and make-believe magic with her friends.

But maybe that's why Brynn looked forward to middle school—she could finally do magic for real. And so, despite the nervousness Brynn felt, there was also excitement and a feeling of anticipation around her. She would finally learn real magic and actually do the things she'd been dreaming of.

Brynn hurried to the kitchen, her mind a swirling vortex of nervousness and eagerness. She fiddled with her food, but didn't eat much.

"A little nervous for school?" asked Dana.

"Nervous?" asked Brynn.

Dana smiled. "Yeah, you barely touched your kelp cakes—your favorite. Need more syrup? What's up?"

"Yeah, I guess I'm a little nervous about school," Brynn admitted. "And magic."

"Mm, I get it," said Brynn's mom. "But you're excited, too, right?"

"About the magic? Yes. About school? Not so much," said Brynn.

Dana nodded, but didn't say anything else. Mermothers often found themselves feeling concerned when their children started going to middle school. Dana had been to middle school, too, of course, and knew that it could be fun and enjoyable. But she also knew that there could be challenges, like the difficulties of learning new subjects. And there were other frustrations, such as dealing with friend issues and even bullies.

"I think you'll like middle school," Dana said after a moment. "But there might be some things you don't like. I hope you'll tell me if there's anything that bothers you."

"Of course I will," said Brynn. She thought it was an odd thing for her mom to say. She always told her mother everything. Brynn nibbled at her breakfast and gave a few bites of kelp cakes to Tully.

"Better take Tully for his walk," said Dana, "or you really will be late."

"Okay," said Brynn. "C'mon, boy! Time for your walk!"

Like most mer-families, Brynn's family lived in an underwater sea cave. It wasn't very big, but Brynn had her own room, so she liked it. Her home was close to where she'd gone to elementary school and to her favorite lagoon, but the middle school was much farther away. She'd have to start riding the speed-current, which was a sort of rapid, undersea river that could be ridden from place to place. This made Brynn nervous, too, because she'd never been on the speed-current by herself, without her parents.

But as Brynn swam with Tully to the surface, she decided to not dwell on those worries for now, and to think only about how middle school meant mer-magic. Tully splashed around at the surface. The merfolk and the fish could breathe underwater, but sea turtles had to surface every four to seven hours to get more air.

Brynn enjoyed going to the surface. The sun shone much brighter above the water and she loved to see the sky. She found it peaceful to look at the sky whether it was a bright day or dark with storm clouds. She loved the sunsets and the stars and clear nights when the moon shone blindingly white.

Sometimes Brynn swam to the surface where the boats and buildings of the humans could be seen in the distance. Brynn never went too close to any humans or their habitations, however. She wouldn't do that even if she were allowed to, which she was not. Brynn had never met a human, never even seen one up close, but she knew they were scary and mean and hated ocean-dwellers. Most of the trash in the ocean came from the humans, and even though Brynn's dad speculated that the humans didn't pollute the ocean on purpose, Brynn wasn't so sure.

Worst of all, some of Brynn's mer-friends had told her that when humans saw mermaids or mermen, they always tried to catch them and keep them locked up. This terrified Brynn, so she stayed far away from the land and from any boats she saw.

As Brynn led Tully back toward home, she said, "Tully, let's stop at our favorite spot. Just for a little while. Then we'll go home, and I'll get ready for school."

Brynn led Tully to the kelp forest. Here, the kelp grew in tall, leafy strands densely spaced on the rocky seafloor. The kelp was long and green and rubbery. Along its length were tough little air bladders that allowed it to float up to the ocean surface to collect sunlight. In the surge of the tide and currents, the kelp swayed hypnotically. Brynn found it relaxing. The kelp could grow a hundred feet tall, and really healthy kelp strands could grow to twice that height.

Brynn swam through the stalks of kelp with Tully at her side. Every now and then she saw the playful sea otters who made the kelp forest their home. The sea otters ate the spiky-shelled sea urchins that crept along the floor of the forest.

"The sea urchins feed on kelp leaves," said Brynn's mother, "and if they were left alone, they'd probably eat up the whole forest."

"But the otters eat the sea urchins?" asked Brynn.

"Right, the otters keep the urchins in check," replied Dana.

"So why don't the otters just eat all the sea urchins?" asked Brynn. "Then the kelp could just grow as much as it wants."

"Well, without the urchins, the kelp would become overgrown," said Dana, "and that's not healthy, either. The urchins eat just enough of the kelp, and the otters each just enough of the sea urchins."

"Who eats the sea otters?" asked Brynn.

"Sea lions and other big predators. That's why the otters need the kelp—to hide from danger. See, there's a balance to the whole kelp forest and the entire sea."

Brynn didn't know it, but this was a kind of mer-magic—the balance of the sea, the way everything in nature worked together, seemingly without really trying.

Mostly, Brynn just loved playing in the vast kelp forest. Hiding among the endless, drifting kelp fronds, getting lost, floating on the mats of vines and leaves at the surface, and just swimming slowly through the filtered sunlight—to Brynn, it was a place of magic.

Within the kelp forest, there was one spot in particular that Brynn thought of as "her" place. It was a small clearing, almost like a room with towering walls made of ever-shifting kelp fronds. At the bottom was a sandy patch of seafloor and a nice rock to sit on. Brynn and Tully came to the clearing. The morning sun was slanting through kelp, flashing and strobing in the current.

"Okay, Tully," said Brynn, "let's make some magic."

She swam around the clearing, clasping her hands and casting pretend spells, like the bubble of protection or the speed burst.

"Someday," she told Tully, "I'm going to be the greatest mermaid alive. I'm going to be able to do all the magic spells. I'll even be able to talk with you."

Tully blinked and seemed to shrug.

Brynn took a deep breath and closed her eyes. She moved her hands together the way she had seen her father when they'd saved Tully from the fishing net. Brynn made sound effects to mimic the mer-magical energy sphere. Then, as she propelled her make-believe magic sphere, a spark flashed from her fingertips. This was followed by a loud crackle. Brynn flinched, then stared at her fingers. Even Tully swam over to investigate.

"Whoa," said Brynn. "Did you see that?"

Tully gazed at Brynn warily. Brynn stretched out her arms and waggled her fingers. There came another spark! Another crackle! Brynn's mouth hung open. She really was a natural! The magic was coming already! It was a spark of real magic, a preview of what was to come. To be able to have done magic with no lessons and without even trying? Brynn thought it must mean that she really was exceptionally gifted, and it reinforced the thought that someday she would be a very talented and skilled mermaid.

From somewhere far away, Brynn heard her mother's voice.

"Bryyyyyynn! Come home! You'll be late, you silly fish!"

"Oops," Brynn mumbled. "We'd better go, Tully."

Tully seemed to nod in agreement. As Brynn stretched out her hand to swim home, there was one last crackle and dazzle of magic sparks.

"Wowee!" said Brynn. "I just can't wait to learn all the spells."

CHAPTER THREE

*O*ver the previous several days, Brynn had tried on several outfits, trying to decide which one she wanted to wear on the first day of school. She wanted to start middle school looking her best and to give a good first impression to the new students and teachers, but now she couldn't decide, so she tried them on all over again. Blouses, hats, and scarves floated around her bedroom

Finally, she picked a top with blue, gold, and green sparkles on it.

"Do you think this complements the scales on my tail, Tully?"

Tully tilted his head, unsure.

"I'll take that as a yes," said Brynn.

She checked herself in the bedroom mirror, smiled, and with Tully close behind, she headed for the kitchen, where she met her father. He'd just gotten out of bed. His hair was messy in the back. He gave Brynn a sleepy wave.

"How come you're up so early, kiddo?"

"Dad," she said. "It's the first day of school!"

"Oh, is that today?" asked Adrian. "I nearly forgot." He winked at Brynn.

"So did she," quipped Brynn's mother. "That mergirl could sleep through a tidal wave."

"I was having a dream about mer-magic!" said Brynn.

"Sounds like you're excited," said Adrian.

Brynn nodded.

"Brynn," said Dana, "do you want me to ride the speed-current with you to school today?"

Brynn thought about this as she pulled on her backpack. If she were being honest, she'd have admitted that she did want her mother to come with her. Or her dad. She'd ridden on the speed-current with her parents a lot—to the library, to the park on the other side of town, to visit friends—but Brynn had never ridden the speed-current on her own. She'd never had to pay attention to how it worked or where it stopped, and she was afraid of getting lost or needing to ask for help. However, she reasoned, she was starting middle school now, and something about that made her feel more grown-up.

"No, that's all right," replied Brynn, trying to sound nonchalant. "I'm going to ride with Jade." She watched her mother's face to see if she looked disappointed, but Dana only nodded.

"Okay," said her mother. "Just pay attention and watch out for traffic."

Brynn patted Tully on the head and gave her parents each a big hug. Then she swam off to meet Jade at the speed-current stop.

Jade was already waiting there when Brynn swam up. Apparently, she'd gotten up early as well. Brynn and Jade had been friends since they were babies. Jade had been born just one day before Brynn. Jade also lived only a few houses away, which meant it was a natural choice for Brynn's first friend.

Jade had beautifully bright white hair, which Brynn had always found a bit perplexing. Brynn had lavender hair, which she'd been told was the result of her father's handsome blue hair and her mother's rich, rose-colored hair. But Jade's mother had flaming red hair and her father had vividly green hair, which Brynn figured should combine to make something like brown hair, not white. But Brynn's mother had explained that hair color, eye color, and other things like personality don't always work the way one might predict.

"We're all individuals," Dana told Brynn when she was very young.

"What's in-vin-diz-ual mean?" asked Brynn.

"In-di-vid-ual," her mother repeated. "It means that even though we all have two eyes and ears and a tail, we're each different and special in our own way."

Regardless, Brynn admired Jade's white hair and the way it sparkled in the water. It contrasted sharply with the deep blue water.

Jade waved hello to Brynn as she swam up.

"You ready for this?" Brynn asked Jade.

"I can't wait," said Jade. "You?"

"Definitely."

"Nervous?" asked Jade.

"No, not at all," said Brynn, even though she felt jellyfish pulsing around in her stomach. "How about you?"

"Nope," said Jade. "Just excited." But Brynn thought that her friend seemed to be fidgeting a little bit more than usual, and that maybe "excited" was just their new word for "terribly nervous."

"Well, then let's go," said Brynn.

The mermaids moved cautiously forward to enter the speed-current, which was rushing by like a river of faster water. Without a single stroke of their tails, the speed-current would take Brynn and Jade to the school very quickly. But it was a little intimidating, too. If you didn't hop on just so, you'd get bumped aside, swirling head over tail. And so they moved carefully forward, pretending to know what they were doing. As they did so, there came a jarring *FOOSH*, and the rush of the speed-current shot them at a high speed through the ocean. The sudden movement startled Brynn. Her eyes opened wide, but she tried to conceal it by quickly putting a smile on her face. She thought she noticed Jade doing the same thing. There were lots of other people on the speed-current. No one seemed to notice the two mermaids, so they tried to avoid looking afraid as they sat down for the ride.

The speed-current wound its way through neighborhoods of merfolk caves. They passed over farms of kelp and seagrass. Then, the speed-current flowed by Brynn's old elementary school. Brynn watched it as they passed. Younger mer-kids filed through the doors with their little backpacks and lunch bags. All of them were dressed in new school clothes and their hair was fixed just so. Brynn happily recalled her years at elementary school, but seeing how the children looked so young, she was reminded that she wasn't a little kid anymore. Brynn looked down at her hands, which just that morning had crackled and flashed with mer-magic. She was definitely ready for middle school.

Inside the speed-current, there weren't just mer-kids on their way to school. Brynn saw all kinds of merfolk—most probably on their way to work. Mixed in with the grown-ups, there were, of course, many young mermaids and merboys who were headed for their first day at Crystal Water Middle School. Brynn recognized a few of the kids from elementary school and wondered if she'd end up in classes with them. She noticed that many of them appeared just a little bit anxious, just like she and Jade were. They stared out at the passing seascape, their eyes wide.

"Look," said Jade, pointing at an older student in front of them. The merboy was creating little sparks of light that floated onto other riders of the speed-current—until they noticed and brushed them away. "That kid knows a little mer-magic."

"Probably in the eighth grade," said Brynn. "That kind of magic is easy. We'll be able to do it soon, no problem."

"You really think so?" asked Jade. "I can't do any magic."

"Ah, it's easy, Jade." Brynn waved her hand dismissively through the water. "I was doing some magic this morning while I took Tully on a walk."

"What?" said Jade, turning to Brynn, her face full of astonishment.

"Yep," replied Brynn, trying to sound bored. "My dad says I'm a natural—I was in the kelp forest just casting a few practice spells before school. You know," she added, "just to warm up."

This, of course, was not entirely true—only a few random sparks of magic had developed, and it had seemed even to Brynn like it was purely accidental.

"Really?" said Jade. "That's amazing! I hope we're in mer-magic classes together so you can tutor me."

Brynn smiled smugly.

A merboy behind them had heard them talking. He made a scoffing sound. Brynn and Jade turned and sat facing him.

"What's your problem?" asked Jade.

"You two. You think magic is gonna be easy?" he said. "It's not. In fact, it's really hard. Probably the hardest subject in school."

Jade scoffed right back at the boy. "This is your first day of middle school, just like us," she said, "so how would you even know?"

"My big brother told me. Said it took him all year just to master the basics."

"Well," replied Jade, "maybe it's hard for your brother, and maybe it'll be hard for you, but Brynn's a natural. She can already do magic."

"Oh yeah?" said the boy. "Then let's see it. Go ahead."

"Show him, Brynn," said Jade.

A chill ran down Brynn's back and into her scales. "Well, sure, okay, but, well, I—"

"Do it, Brynn," urged Jade, nudging her with an elbow. "Cast a stun spell and shock this kid right in the tail."

"Um, well, okay, but—"

"What's the matter?" the merboy chided. "Can you cast spells or not?"

"A few," said Brynn, "but our stop is coming up." She pointed.

They were approaching a sign that stood above the speed-current. It signaled the stop for Crystal Waters Middle School. Jade and Brynn turned around to gather their things and put on their backpacks. Then they hopped off the speed-current.

"Who is that kid?" Brynn whispered to Jade as they swam toward the school.

"His name's William Beach. I went to summer camp with him. I don't think he's got any friends, and he's super annoying."

The two mermaids joined the other children. There were so many of them, all flooding in the same direction. The tide of mer-students carried Brynn and Jade along to the grounds of the middle school, a sprawling, three-story complex of cave classrooms, hallways, gymnasiums, auditoriums, and courtyards. Brynn and Jade were quiet as they swam through the massive front entrance. This school was at least ten times larger than their elementary school. It was almost like a small town! Brynn wondered if she'd have enough time to get from one class to the next. Or would she simply get lost right away and never even make it to class?

Within the cavernous school, with all the noise and unfamiliar faces surrounding her, Brynn felt her heart quicken.

"Hey," she said to Jade with puffed-up confidence, "let me see your schedule, and I'll help you find our classes." In reality, Brynn was hoping that she had first period with Jade so that they could stay together a little longer. It would be so bizarre this year: a different teacher for each subject, having to race around to different classrooms, each one full of different kids. Brynn had been so excited to start learning magic, but she was beginning to realize how scary it might be. And what would she do if she couldn't go through it all with her best friend?

Jade dug around in her backpack and the mermaids compared schedules. Brynn's day started with language arts with Key Wallace. Next came math with Shelley Smith, followed by science with Gill Denny, social studies with John Poole, singing with Betty Barnacle, and then—finally—the class Brynn was most excited for, Introduction to Magic with Windy Meyers.

"Jade," exclaimed Brynn. "We don't have a single class together!"

"At least we'll have lunch together," said Jade.

Brynn sighed. "Yeah," she said sadly, adjusting her backpack strap. "But that's not very long."

"We better go," said Jade. "We still need to find our classes, and it's almost time for school to start."

"Okay," pouted Brynn. "I'll save you a seat in the lunchroom."

Jade thanked Brynn and swam away. Brynn watched Jade go but soon lost sight of her in the crowd of students. Brynn examined her class schedule, trying to figure out where her first class was, but there were so many students and so many hallways. She looked at her map of the school, but she couldn't get her bearings. The map seemed to be upside down and backward no matter which way she turned it.

The flow of traffic jostled Brynn and spun her around. Everyone else seemed to know where to go, so Brynn did the same, pretending she was going just where she aimed to. She followed the crowd down one hallway and then up another, but to her, every area looked identical. After a few minutes, she was certain she was hopelessly lost.

Brynn hadn't even made it to her first class, and already she was almost crying. The first bell rang, and Brynn felt a heavy wave of anxiety crash around her.

Just then, a teacher swam up to Brynn's side. She had beautiful yellow hair, and she carried a clipboard. "Can I help you find your class?" she asked Brynn. Her voice was calm, and this immediately eased Brynn's anxiety a little.

"Who me?" said Brynn. "Nah. I'm not lost." She tried acting like a seventh-grader or even an eighth-grader, but she wasn't sure how older kids acted, so she just pretended like nothing mattered to her.

"Ah, I'm relieved to hear that," said the teacher with a smile.

Brynn could see why this teacher had been assigned to help out the kids who got lost—her voice and attitude were really quite soothing.

The teacher added, "Most of the students get at least a little lost on the first day of middle school."

"Oh, really?" asked Brynn.

"Sure," said the teacher, swimming alongside Brynn. "This school is enormous! The map is confusing, and have you noticed how all the hallways look a lot alike?"

"Yes!" cried Brynn, but then she checked herself. "I mean—yeah, I guess."

"Even the seventh- and eighth-graders get a little turned around. In fact, are you completely sure you're on the right course, because I just now realized that there are only ninth-grade classes in this hallway, and unless I'm mistaken, you're in sixth grade."

"Is it that obvious?" Brynn said gloomily.

"Well," the teacher went on, "if I had to guess just based on your confidence, I'd say you were in eighth grade. Maybe ninth."

Brynn grinned and then went back to looking like she didn't care about anything.

"But," said the teacher, "I've taught here for several years, and if you'd been here last year, I would have remembered your lovely, long lavender hair! What's your name?"

"Brynn Finley!" cried Brynn, and with the last of her nervousness melting away, a fountain of words poured from her lips, practically without any permission. "My mom's hair is rose-tinted and my dad's hair is blue, so my hair is lavender but my best friend's hair is pure white because we're all individuals, and my dad says I'm a natural because I calmed down a baby sea turtle a few weeks ago."

The teacher took a moment to process the jumble of words. Then she said, "Let's have a look at that schedule. Ah, yes, Miss Wallace's class. It's this way. I'll show you." The beautiful teacher led the way, and Brynn followed her. "I'm Mrs. Meyers," said the teacher. "But you can call me Windy."

"You teach magic!" said Brynn, looking at Mrs. Meyers with undisguised awe.

"Yes, and I recognize your name, Brynn. I'll see you in class later today. All right, here's your classroom. Have a good first day!"

Brynn had been excited for magic class since the end of the last school year, but now that she knew that Mrs. Meyers was such a nice teacher, she was even more excited. As the roll was called for language arts, she was already daydreaming about Mrs. Meyers's class.

"Wow," said Mrs. Meyers in the daydream, "you really are a natural, aren't you, Brynn Finley? Finley? Finley? Has anyone seen Brynn Finley?"

Roll call!

"Oh!" cried Brynn, raising her hand and waving it frantically. "Here! I'm here!"

By lunchtime, Brynn felt worn out. In every class, they recited rules, reviewed syllabuses, and passed around papers for parents to sign. It was over-whelming and tedious at the same time. And not only did Brynn not have Jade to keep her company, she didn't really know any of the other students in her classes.

Brynn swam uncertainly into the chaos of the lunchroom. There seemed to be a thousand mer-kids there, all competing for food and places to sit. Brynn picked up a lunch tray and made her way through the slow, rushing confusion of the lunch line. She got her lunch safely through the line without spilling it all over herself, barely, but then she remembered she was supposed to save a seat for Jade. There were almost no seats for one person to sit, let alone two.

To her great relief, she saw that Jade was already there and had saved Brynn a seat. Jade smiled and waved at Brynn. With a few weary wags of her tail, Brynn drifted across the room and sat down across from her friend.

"Well, how's it going?" asked Jade warily.

"I don't know about this," said Brynn. "So far, middle school is just like fifth grade, times seven classes, minus recess."

"I know what you mean," said Jade. "I don't know a single person in any of my classes."

"I'm still holding out for magic class, but it's not until the end of the day!" huffed Brynn. She picked at her lunch—fish sticks with macaroni and seaweed—

but before Brynn could take even a few bites, the bell rang, sending everyone back to class.

"That's it?" Brynn moaned. "That's all the time we get to eat?"

Jade shrugged forlornly. "Hang in there," she said to Brynn.

"You, too," said Brynn, trying to wolf down a little food as she gathered up her lunch tray.

CHAPTER FOUR

*A*fter what felt like forever, it was at last time for Brynn's final class of the day, Introduction to Magic.

Unfortunately, by then, Brynn was exhausted. The stress of the big new school, the loud and crowded hallways, and the many new faces had drained most of Brynn's emotional energy. All she wanted now was to go home and take Tully for a quick walk and then maybe a nap!

And so she swam slowly into Mrs. Meyers' classroom. Other mer-kids were horsing around and chattering about their big first day at school. Brynn mostly ignored them. She drifted unsteadily through the water and slumped into one of the rocky slabs that served as classroom desks. More and more students crammed into the room. Sitting still for a few moments felt heavenly to Brynn, but she became slowly aware that someone was looking her way. Brynn looked around and saw William Beach, the merboy from the speed-current, sitting next to her, watching her, and wearing what Brynn took to be a snarky grin.

When Mrs. Meyers (or Windy, as she apparently liked to be called) swam into the classroom, a smile on her bright and friendly face, the students settled down and Brynn perked up. Brynn had decided that she wanted to be just like Windy when she grew up: kind but confident; poised and smart. As a naturally apt magic pupil, Brynn thought, she herself should probably go into teaching—it would be her responsibility to help the mer-kids coming up behind her. Brynn was even thinking that maybe she herself might be a magic teacher. And even though it was still just the very first day, Brynn was certain that Introduction to Magic with Mrs. Windy Meyers was going to be her favorite class.

As Windy passed by Brynn's desk, she leaned over to Brynn and whispered, "I see you had no problem finding your final class! Good to see you again!"

Brynn couldn't think of anything to say, so she simply grinned back.

Windy began with a thorough discussion of all the class rules. Brynn tried to pay attention, but she wanted to hear about mer-magic. As the class wore on and Windy got all the boring stuff out of the way, she told them a little bit about what they would be learning that year.

Windy said, "You're going to learn some basic magic, including some speed spells, a few spells to create light, and some energy spells."

"I could use an energy spell right about now," Brynn muttered to herself.

"We might even get into some early healing spells," Windy added.

The students in class murmured with anticipation.

"I'm glad you're so excited," said Windy, nodding. "By the time you finish this class, you might be able to heal small injuries."

"What, like a paper cut?" quipped William Beach.

Windy chuckled. "I suppose it could be used on a paper cut, but generally, that's not the kind of injury that requires magic. The first spells you learn won't be super powerful, but this one could help with small cuts and bruises."

Even though it was the end of the day, Windy easily held the class's attention. Brynn realized that the other students were just as excited to learn to do magic as she was. It made sense—most merfolk were proud of their responsibility to protect life in the ocean. The students had spent their whole lives watching the adults use magic to help others. It wasn't surprising then that the children wanted to participate.

Windy continued. "The things you learn in this class will eventually help you to fulfill the merfolk oath." She pointed to a banner hung on the wall and read it to them.

I am a protector of the ocean, a guardian of the sea. Wherever living things need help, that's where I'll be.

Windy went on, explaining that the first step of learning magic was to be able to take the love you feel in your heart and form it into energy.

"This is one of those things," explained Windy, "that I like to describe as simple, but not easy. All you'll be doing is converting your love in your heart into a little ball of energy, but it will be different from anything you've done before. That love, that little energy ball is the foundation for every magical mer-spell you will ever cast."

Brynn thought back to the moment in the kelp forest when, without even trying, sparks of magic had flowed from her fingertips. It wasn't just luck—it was love! Her love of her little clearing in the kelp forest had turned into magic right before her eyes. Maybe, Brynn thought, the other kids in the class would struggle with this, but Brynn had no doubt it would come to her quite easily. Despite what Windy told the class, Brynn knew that it would be simple *and* easy. She smiled, then she glanced over at William and thought she detected confusion and worry in his face. He'd probably struggle a lot, thought Brynn. She'd heard that certain merfolk were unable to do magic, but she'd never met someone like that. But what would a merperson even do if they couldn't do magic? Brynn shook her head. She couldn't even imagine. Maybe that's what William would turn out to be—one of these non-magical merfolk. Brynn made a mental note to inform Mrs. Meyers—Windy—that, as a naturally gifted student of mer-magic, she'd be perfectly happy to be the class tutor and help the slower students such as William.

Just then, Brynn realized the entire class was looking at her.

"Brynn?" chimed Windy. "Did you hear the question?"

Brynn's eyes darted around. "Who, me? Oh! Yes! I heard it. But could you maybe repeat it? Just so I can, you know, give the clearest possible answer?"

For some reason, the other students sniggered at this.

"Hm," said Windy with an odd smile. "Certainly. Just as a review of the class rules, I asked what you should do if we're having quiet reading time and you need to get a drink or visit the bathroom?"

The students laughed again.

"Oh, uhm, right," said Brynn. "I should raise my hand."

"That's close," said Windy. "What I'd prefer is that you quietly approach my desk and ask quietly to leave the room. That way, I won't have to call on you and disrupt the class."

"Right," said Brynn. "Of course." She looked at William and caught him rolling his eyes.

"Well, we still have some time left," Windy said. "So how about we get started with your very first spell?"

Brynn sat up, paying careful attention. They were going to do a spell on their very first day? Brynn couldn't believe it.

"Everyone, close your eyes," said Windy.

The classroom fell quiet, and Brynn and the other students closed their eyes.

"Think about your loved ones. And think about the places you love to go."

Brynn pictured her father and mother, and then she thought of Jade and Tully. She pictured her clearing in the forest and the way the diffused sunlight played in the tall, waving strands of kelp. These thoughts made her feel very calm and peaceful.

"Keep those thoughts in your mind," said Windy, "and while you do, cup your hands, like you're holding a small stone."

Brynn cupped her hands just like her parents did when casting spells.

"Now," said Windy, "take a deep breath, and concentrate on your feelings and images. You should feel a kind of humming sensation. Some people say it's a buzz."

Brynn focused on her thoughts and the pictures in

her mind, but she didn't feel any buzzing or humming.

Windy said, "Now, I know this sounds kinda strange, but direct that buzz or hum outward, to your arms and then your hands."

Even though Brynn thought she was doing what the teacher had instructed, nothing happened. She heard the crackle of magic, just as she'd heard it that morning in the kelp forest, but it was coming from elsewhere. A few gasps of delight could be heard in the room.

"Keep trying," said Windy. "You're all doing great!"

Brynn peeked at her fingers, just in case there was something there, but there was nothing. She furrowed her brow and tried harder, but still nothing happened. The more she tried to do the spell, the less peaceful she felt, until she couldn't even hold the vision of the kelp forest in her mind. Now she didn't feel calm at all; just agitated and anxious.

After a couple of minutes, the room was quiet.

"Were you able to feel anything?" asked Windy. "Any tingle or slight vibration? You don't have to raise your hand if you don't want to."

A few students nodded, and William of all people raised his hand. He turned to Brynn and smiled.

"It's all right if you didn't," Windy continued in her easy-going way. "I would be very surprised if you were all able to conjure on your first day. *The first*

A.M. LUZZADER

day is the worst day. That's what I always tell my students. This is something that's going to take time, so don't get discouraged. I'm proud of all of you for giving it a good try. You are going to learn wonderful things this year and every single one of you will be able to do this spell soon. I guarantee it."

Despite her teacher's words, Brynn was crestfallen. Maybe it was all right that some of the other students hadn't been able to do any magic, but she expected more from herself. She was a natural! Her father said so.

For the rest of the week, the class spent every day working on conjuring the energy sphere. Windy told them to practice at home. Brynn practiced almost all the time—at school, at lunch, on the speed-current, and even in bed.

By the third day of class, several more students were able to successfully conjure the little spheres of sparks that would eventually become spells of light, healing, and power. None were any bigger than a turtle egg, but William Beach could now whip up a basic mer-magic sphere without appearing to try very hard.

Brynn felt a great weight pressing down on her. The more she practiced, the more she felt discouraged. She couldn't even feel the subtle humming sensation that Windy told them they'd feel.

One evening, Brynn sat in her room, determined to finally make her mer-magic work. She tried and

48

tried and tried, until she again felt so agitated that love and passion were the farthest emotions from her mind. After what Brynn guessed was her one-thousandth attempt, she lost her temper and grabbed the closest object at hand—it happened to be her school backpack—and she slammed it angrily on the floor. Books, papers, and pencils spilled out and then swirled around Brynn's room, as though it were some kind of school-themed snow globe.

Tully raced out of the room. A minute later, Brynn's dad poked his head into the bedroom.

"Everything okay in here?" he asked, looking quizzically at her homework and schoolbooks floating around.

"Uh, yeah," said Brynn. "Just, uh, doing some cleaning up."

"Oh, okay," said Adrian. "Hey, how's school going? How's magic class? I've heard that Mrs. Meyers is a fantastic teacher."

Brynn licked her lips. She didn't want her father to know that she wasn't doing well. She was frustrated as it was and didn't think she could deal with her dad's disappointment.

"Great, Dad," Brynn said. "Me and Chelsea were the first in the class to do the illumination spell," Brynn lied.

"Really?" exclaimed Adrian. "That's fantastic! After only a few days? That's incredible! Wow. You know, after seeing you with Tully that day on the reef, I had a feeling you'd be a natural, but I didn't want to tell you right away. You know—I didn't want you to feel any pressure. But I'm proud of you, Brynn. You'll be doing better magic than me pretty soon."

By that point, Brynn just wanted him to go away.

"Hey! Why don't I get your mom and you can show us!"

Brynn's heart sank. "Uhm, well, I, the thing is—"

"Hold on," said Adrian. "I'll get her."

"No, Dad," Brynn said. "See, the truth is—"

"What's the matter, hon?"

"Well, the truth is—I should be working on my social studies homework right now."

"Ohhh," her dad said. "Oh, right. Yeah, mer-magic's important, but it's not the only subject. Right. You're smart, kiddo. Okay. I'll leave you alone. You study." He gave Brynn two thumbs up and then hurried out of her bedroom.

Brynn felt awful for lying, but she told herself that if she could just figure out the illumination spell—or any spell, for that matter—she would certainly move to the head of the class and impress her parents. Then would a little fib matter so much?

"I'll try harder," Brynn told herself, "and things will get better."

Things got worse.

By the end of the week, all the other students in the class had successfully completed the illumination spell, and William had become Windy's in-class tutor.

"Hey, Brynn," he asked her. "You want me to help you with your conjuring?"

"No," she said firmly. "I can do it just fine on my own. I did it at home just this morning. Several times."

On Friday, in magic class, Windy directed all of the students to practice the illumination spell. Brynn tried a couple times, but when she still wasn't able to do it, she folded her arms in her lap and hoped no one would notice her.

Windy swam around the room, checking on the students' progress and correcting hand positions.

"You guys are doing so well," she said. "I'm very proud of you all. Now, before we move on, is there anyone who hasn't been able to conjure the illumination spell? Anyone who needs more help? It's okay if you do—this stuff isn't easy! Anyone?"

William looked over at Brynn with a questioning expression. He may have intended to be helpful, but to Brynn, it felt like he was mocking her. She shot William a hard scowl, and he looked away.

Brynn's conscience practically screamed at her to raise her hand and ask for help, but there was a stronger impulse: avoid embarrassment at all costs. So, she said nothing. How had it come to this? Brynn honestly could not believe she was the only one in class who couldn't do it. There had to be an explanation. Maybe she was getting sick. Maybe it was because sitting next to William gave her bad vibes.

"Everyone's got it? Tracey? Brynn? You mermaids got it?" Windy checked.

Brynn felt William's gaze on her, but she nodded anyway.

"That's great!" cried Windy. "Class, I'm so proud of you! On Monday, we'll move on to the next spell! Keep practicing your illumination spell, though, because it's the base for all the spells we'll learn this semester."

Now there's no other option, Brynn thought. *Now I'll have to learn how to do it this weekend on my own.*

As Brynn and Jade sat on the speed-current that afternoon, Brynn turned everything over in her mind. What was she doing wrong? What was she missing?

Jade nudged her. "Hey, what's wrong? You've been like a clam all week."

"Oh, I'm fine," muttered Brynn. "Just thinking about magic class." Brynn was just about to swallow her pride and ask Jade to help her learn the illumination spell, but before she could, Jade interrupted her.

"Isn't it so fun?" cried Jade. "I didn't believe you when you said it would be easy, but now we're both conjuring mer-magic and casting illumination spells. I mean, I know you probably did it on your first try, but I got it to work on Tuesday. It wasn't easy, but I did it, Brynn! You were right!"

"That's great," said Brynn through her gritted teeth.

"I just wish I could be in class with you," said Jade with a wistful sigh. "We'd be great together, and I've heard Meyers is the best!"

Brynn knew she should be happy for her friend, but knowing how easy it was for Jade made Brynn feel even worse. She felt tears start from her eyes, but living in the ocean as mermaids did, it was always a bit difficult to know if someone was crying. Meanwhile, Jade jabbered all the way home about how fun it was to learn mer-magic. And now if she admitted to Jade that she couldn't do the spell, Brynn knew she would break down into a full sobbing fit, and she didn't want everyone on the crowded speed-current to see that.

"I think we're gonna be the two greatest mermaids ever, Brynn. I'm so glad we're friends."

As soon as she got off the speed-current, Brynn hurried home. She wanted to be alone as soon as possible so that she could calm herself down and practice the illumination spell. She meant to head straight to her room, but as she came through the door, Brynn's mom looked up from a book she was reading and saw her. There must have been something about the way Brynn looked—maybe a worried expression or the almost-invisible tears in her eyes—because instead of saying hello, the first words Dana said to her were, "Brynn, what's wrong?"

"Nothing, nothing," Brynn shouted as she dove for her room. She shut her bedroom door and slid into her bed. Tully sniffed around, confused. She pulled the turtle close to her as she cried.

Her mother knocked at the door. "Brynn," she said without coming in, "is everything okay?"

"I'm fine, Mom," she called, her voice cracking. "I just need some time alone."

Her mother was quiet for a moment. She still didn't open the door.

"Wanna talk about it later?"

"Sure, Mom. Yeah. Later."

"Okay, then. Come find me when you're ready." Brynn could hear the concern in her mother's voice.

"She's already worried, and she doesn't even know why yet," Brynn whispered to Tully. "If I tell her I'm the only one in the class who can't do even the simplest of spells, she'll really worry. We can't tell anyone, Tully. It's too embarrassing." Brynn sniffed and more tears came from her eyes, mixing with the seawater. "I'll figure it out tomorrow, though. Whatever it takes. I won't stop until I can do that stupid spell."

CHAPTER FIVE

L ater that night, Brynn told her mother that she wasn't feeling well.

"That's why I was crying," Brynn said. "It was a bad stomach ache. Maybe it was the school lunch."

It was another lie.

"Oh, really?" her mother asked. "Not a fan of the cafeteria food, huh? I always liked it. Especially the fish sticks. I guess you take after your father, the food snob. If you want to bring a sack lunch, I'm sure your dad will make you something delicious."

"Okay," said Brynn, but of course, she wasn't worried about what she ate for lunch. The lies seemed to be piling up, but Brynn couldn't see any other option. It was too humiliating, too shameful, she thought, to admit that she couldn't do the spell.

She started to think that she was different from the other merpeople, and she didn't like it. What if she were one of those merpeople who couldn't do magic?

Early Saturday morning, she told her parents she was taking Tully out for his walk.

But after they surfaced, instead of going back home, Brynn took Tully to the kelp forest with the plan to stay there until she could do the illumination spell. Had she imagined those sparks of mer-magic jumping from her fingers on the first day of school? No! Magic had happened in the kelp forest before, she was sure of it, and it could happen again, even if it had been an accident. Brynn was hopeful that whatever it was in the kelp forest that had made it so she could do magic before could help her to do this spell.

When Brynn and Tully reached her peaceful little clearing, Brynn realized they weren't alone.

She heard a woman shouting nearby. Shouting angrily.

Tully huddled behind Brynn's tailfin.

"Wait here, Tully," said Brynn. She ventured out of the clearing, swimming from one kelp stalk to the next in the direction of the commotion. Soon she came to the edge of the kelp forest. Brynn peered out from among the kelp stalks.

It was Phaedra.

The sea witch, they called her. She was not a mermaid, not of the merfolk at all, but some other sort of being. She had legs like a human instead of a tailfin, and her hands and feet were webbed for swimming. The sea witch was able to breathe water and live in the sea, and rumor had it she knew powerful magic.

"Dark magic," Jade had once called it. "The bad kind."

Brynn didn't know what dark magic was, but she didn't want to find out, either. She only knew that while mer-magic was powered by love, dark magic came from somewhere else. She cowered in the kelp.

Brynn had never seen Phaedra before, but she'd heard that the sea witch was beautiful. Even from a distance, Brynn could now see that "beautiful" really wasn't the word. Phaedra was stunning, breathtaking. Her skin was lustrous, like a pearl or the inside of an abalone shell. Phaedra's hair was long, black, and straight. Her lips were blood red, and her eyes were dark and moody. Jade had once told Brynn that the sea witch used her dark magic to make herself appear beautiful and to stay that way forever. Brynn had asked her mother if that were true.

"Well, I don't know Phaedra personally," said her mother, "but it's not polite to spread rumors."

Phaedra floated majestically in the water at the edge of the kelp forest. She was shouting at a dagon.

The dagons were a race of fish people who supposedly came from the very deepest bottoms of the sea. They had legs and arms like humans, but they were covered with green scales and their hands and feet resembled fins, and they had gills on their cheeks. Brynn didn't know any dagons personally, and there weren't many of them around Fulgent, the town where Brynn lived. Most dagons lived far away from the merfolk. Brynn assumed they had their own towns and schools, but she didn't really know. Brynn didn't know much about dagons at all, but her impression was they weren't very nice. She thought of them as bullies, though she wasn't sure why— she'd never been bullied by a dagon and didn't know anyone who had.

"You listen to me, Ian Fletcher, it must be done today!" Phaedra shouted at the dagon. "Not tomorrow, not next week. Today. Do you understand me?"

The dagon bowed. "Yes, Phaedra. It will be done."

Brynn was annoyed and frightened that the sea witch chose the kelp forest to yell at this poor dagon, but she wondered what they were up to. She strained to hear what they were saying, leaning forward to see what they were doing.

Just then, Brynn felt something tugging at her tail. She turned to see. It was Tully. The little turtle's eyes held a fearful expression and he pulled at her with his beak, as though to keep her away from the sea witch.

"Tully, go back," whispered Brynn. "Go back to the clearing and wait for me!"

The sea witch had been telling the cowering dagon how much trouble he'd be in if her orders were not carried out, but now she paused and turned her head.

Brynn tried to be still, but Tully kept tugging at her. Brynn wrestled her tail away from Tully, but in doing so, she burst out from the kelp, and the sea witch saw her.

Keeping her eyes on Brynn, the sea witch said, "Be gone, Ian Fletcher."

The dagon made a pitiful little bow, turned, and swam quickly away. He was soon lost from Brynn's view. Phaedra, on the other hand, leveled a cool, malevolent gaze at Brynn and held it for a few seconds. Brynn even saw the sea witch raise an eyebrow at her. Brynn's heart began to thump in her chest.

And then Phaedra vanished in a vaporous cloud as black as the ink of a giant squid.

In another moment, there was only empty water.

Brynn looked around. Tully huddled next to her, his big eyes darting here and there.

"I guess they left," said Brynn, not exactly sure whether to be relieved or frightened. "Well, I guess I can try some magic practice now," she said. "C'mon, Tully, let's go back to the clearing."

However, before they'd gone very far, Brynn was feeling almost as edgy as Tully was acting. Back in the clearing, Brynn's heart raced and her hands trembled. She couldn't focus on love or passion or peace. But because they were there at the kelp forest, Brynn could at least focus on the dreamily flowing kelp, so she tried that. She took a few deep breaths, and pictured her dad, with his blue hair and glasses and his dad jokes. "Say, Brynn, what'd the ocean say to the beach? Nothing. Just waved." The jokes weren't very funny, but that cracked Adrian up. He had a full, hearty laugh that sometimes made him double over. Brynn loved to hear her dad laugh.

Next, Brynn tried to focus on her mom. She seemed to always detect how Brynn was feeling—Brynn almost never had to even tell her. Brynn's mom was also really good at cheering Brynn up when she was sad. If Brynn were having a bad day, her mom would surprise Brynn with three-shrimp-salad or some other favorite food. Brynn's mom was also super intelligent, always seemed to know the answer to every problem, and always made Brynn feel very safe.

Even though Tully was a fairly new addition to Brynn's life, Brynn thought of him as part of the family. When Brynn was happy, no one was more fun to play with than Tully—playing fetch or just swimming along in the ocean. And when Brynn was sad, like she had been lately, Tully always snuggled up to her. Other people occurred to Brynn—her grandparents and her best friend, Jade, and even her magic teacher, Windy Meyers.

She didn't really notice it distinctly, but some of the tension in Brynn's shoulders eased. She was breathing more deeply and cupping her hands in a relaxed, natural way. Without thinking too intensely about it, Brynn moved the positive energy she felt outward, into her arms, into her hands, down to her fingers, and then she felt the slightest tickle or tingle, a gentle thrumming or humming sensation. She opened her eyes and looked down at her cupped hands.

There was nothing. No sphere of light. Not even a few sparks of mer-magical energy.

"Ugh!" Brynn whined in frustration.

She tried again. And again. And again.

It was nearly lunchtime, and aside from the pleasant trilling of positive energy she first felt, Brynn still hadn't been able to conjure any mer-magic, not even there in the kelp clearing, the most magical place Brynn knew. Tully lay in the sand, napping. He'd need to go to the surface soon, and Brynn knew her parents would be expecting her home, too.

She decided to try again just once more.

Just as she began to slow her breathing and focus on her positive feelings, it all fell apart when she heard the sound of snide laughter. She opened her eyes. The dagon she'd seen earlier was swimming toward her through the kelp. She'd heard the sea witch call him by a name. What was it? Eric? Igor? Ian!

As he came into the clearing, he smiled, revealing rows of sharp, pointed teeth.

"Well, well, well," said Ian, circling Brynn, "who's this?"

"Leave me alone," said Brynn, moving closer to Tully.

"All right. But let me ask you a question," said Ian. His voice was deep and buzzy. "If a mermaid can't do magic, is she really even a mermaid?"

"I *can* do magic," said Brynn defensively.

"Is that what you're doing here?" Ian asked, looking around. "Because I've been watching you for quite a while now, and while it's been amusing, I wouldn't say it's been—magical." He chuckled and swam closer. They were almost face to face.

"I'm still a kid," she said.

"Oh, but you should be learning magic by now, shouldn't you?"

"How is that any of your business," asked Brynn.

The dagon shrugged and began swimming away. "I suppose it's not," he said. "I was only trying to help you."

"Help me? Help me how?" Brynn asked.

"Too late," said Ian as he pushed off from the ocean floor. "I've changed my mind."

The encounter had woken Tully, who swam close

to Brynn's side. "He's lying," Brynn told Tully. "He couldn't help me. Dagons don't even do magic."

But Brynn was getting desperate, and if there had been some way for the dagon to have helped her, she knew she wouldn't be opposed to it.

CHAPTER SIX

*B*rynn was so worried about whether she'd be able to do the magic spell in Windy's class, she couldn't focus on her other classes. Her stomach hurt like she had swallowed a spiky stonefish. The feeling of dread stayed with her the whole day, even during the lunch break.

"Hey," said Jade at lunch, "do you want to go look for sea glass to make necklaces on Saturday?"

"Hmm? What?" said Brynn. All she could think of was how she couldn't do magic. She wasn't even sure what Jade had been saying.

"What's with you?" Jade asked. "You don't seem like yourself. You haven't eaten any of your lunch, and you're acting like I'm not even here."

"Oh, sorry," Brynn mumbled. "I was just thinking about—the coral reef."

"The coral reef? What about it?"

"Um, just that it's pretty. That's all," said Brynn. She was relieved when the bell rang. It was too hard trying to act like everything was fine and to be interested in other things when she was so worried about her magic class.

The magic class had moved on to conjuring other magic, like simple healing spells. But because Brynn couldn't form the beginner's energy sphere, there was no way she could do these other spells. So, she fiddled around in class, pretending to take notes, searching for something in her backpack, or going to the bathroom.

William would sometimes offer to help Brynn, and he was probably trying to be genuinely nice, but to Brynn, it was all just so humiliating to think of getting so far behind in a class where she'd actually claimed to be naturally gifted on the very first day of school.

"Hey, Brynn," said William. "Want to practice the energy sphere with me?"

"No thanks," said Brynn. "This class is actually kind of boring me because it's going so slow."

And so Brynn generally tried to stay out of sight, but she knew she was falling farther and farther behind, and it seemed like there was no way to ever catch up. She was also certain that Windy had figured out she couldn't do magic, or that she would soon, and although Brynn was afraid and ashamed, a part of her was aching to be caught so that she didn't have to keep up the fakery. So Brynn wasn't sure what to think when Mrs. Meyers asked her to stay after class.

As the other mer-students filed out of the classroom, Brynn approached Mrs. Meyers' desk. It wasn't really a desk, but more like a big mossy boulder with lots of small holes and little nooks to hold papers and pencils and paper clips.

"Mrs. Meyers? You wanted to talk to me?" asked Brynn.

"Yes," said Windy, setting down her pen. "I wanted to talk to you about your magic. I noticed you haven't been participating in class. Are you having a hard time? Do you need help?"

For a moment, Brynn thought about confessing everything. Mrs. Meyers was so nice. She'd understand, wouldn't she?

But then again, she wanted Windy to like her. If she told Windy that she couldn't do the very beginning spell, the one everyone else could do, Windy would probably think she was stupid, and then Windy probably wouldn't pay attention to her.

"Need help? Oh, no, not me," said Brynn. "It's pretty easy stuff. In fact, I've been a little bored. That's why I haven't been participating much. Some of the other kids might be struggling, though. Like Will. He could probably use some help."

Windy looked at Brynn for a moment, as though she maybe saw the truth behind Brynn's words.

Windy was the type of teacher who cared immensely about her students. Being a teacher wasn't something she took lightly. She was a teacher because she loved children and wanted to see them succeed. Windy believed that every student had boundless potential, and with a little help, they could all be successful. She was especially glad to be a magic teacher because it allowed her to teach the students about their special magical abilities, which they would use throughout their lives. She was worried about Brynn because it didn't seem like she was understanding the material.

"Well, if you ever need help, Brynn, that's what I'm here for. I'm your teacher, and I can help you." She rose from her chair and began cleaning the chalkboard. "Not everything comes easily," she continued. "Even the brightest and smartest students sometimes have to work extra hard at certain stages. And sometimes students get so anxious about doing well that they can't relax enough to be able to do magic. It's a balancing act. Magic isn't just about knowing the physical steps to doing a spell, it's also about being able to manage your feelings internally. You have to keep yourself from thinking about the mistakes you've made in the past or your worries or hopes for the future and to just concentrate on working through the spell. Sometimes it helps just to try to relax and focus on taking deep breaths."

"That's nice," said Brynn, trying hard to hold the

casual smile on her face, "but like I said, I'm doing great."

"Okay," said Windy, setting down the eraser. "You want to do some magic now? With me? We could practice a little?"

"Well, I should be honest with you, Mrs. Meyers," said Brynn. She bit her lip and thought about what to say next. "It's just that the school days are so long, and I'm pretty tired. And besides, I gotta go catch the speed-current. I need to get home. To walk my turtle."

"But, Brynn—"

"Yeah, gotta go," said Brynn as she swam through the door.

"Okay," Windy called after her, "but just remember, I'm here if you need me! Midterms are coming up!"

The halls of the school were practically deserted, with most of the students already hopping on the speed-current to head home. Brynn leaned against the wall, trying to catch her breath. Could Mrs. Meyers tell that she was lying? She hoped not. But she had to do something soon, especially with the midterms coming up. She couldn't keep faking it, not for long anyway. Somehow, she had to figure out this problem.

At dinner that night, Brynn poked at her food. Her parents had been talking about something or other, but she hadn't been listening. But then, their attention turned to her.

"So, Brynn," said her dad, "how's school going?"

"School? School's great. Yeah, really good."

"That's wonderful," said her mom. "What's your favorite subject this year?"

"Favorite subject? Um, yeah, I guess that would be language arts. Gotta love those books. *Old Sheller, Anne of Green Groupers, A Winkle in Time.*"

"I would have thought you'd say Intro to Magic," said her dad. "You were so excited about it before school began."

"Magic?" Brynn felt her face turning red. She shifted uncomfortably in her chair.

"Yeah," said her father. "You've been so eager to learn magic. It was always my favorite subject."

"Mine, too," said her mom with a fond grin.

"Oh, well, yeah, I mean, if I'm allowed to pick that as my favorite, then yeah, magic is great."

"What have you been learning?" asked her mom.

"All kinds of things," said Brynn with a sigh. "But mostly we're sticking with basic illumination and healing. You know, some of the kids are kind of struggling with it, though." Brynn looked at her parents to see how they would respond. In a way, she hoped they would realize that she was talking about herself, but she was just a little too insecure to just come out and say she needed help. Would they be able to tell?

"Oh, I'm sure these classmates of yours will figure it out. I'm just glad you're doing well with it," said her father. "Honey, can you pass some more sea greens?"

Brynn's shoulders slumped. *They only want me to do well*, Brynn thought, *and they definitely wouldn't want to know that I couldn't conjure.*

Brynn's mother passed a bowl of greens to her father.

"Oh, yeah. I'm actually the best in the class," said Brynn.

Her parents had a brief look of surprise on their faces, but then they both smiled.

"Brynn, that's terrific! I'll have to send news to your grandparents," said her mom. "They'll want to hear this."

"Uh," said Brynn, her heart beginning to pound again.

Why couldn't she just come out and tell them? She wanted to, but every time she got ready to form the words, she pushed the thought aside.

"Show us something," her father urged.

"Show you something?" said Brynn, frozen suddenly with fear.

"Yeah," her father continued with a friendly smile. "Just a little something. Anything."

Brynn pushed away from the table. "Maybe later," she said, only barely concealing her panic. "I just remembered I need to take Tully for his walk," she said. "Gotta go! Bye!" She didn't excuse herself or even clear her plate. "Tully! Come on, Tully! Time for your walk! Let's go, boy!"

Tully had been on a walk just before dinner, but he gladly came to Brynn's side, and together, they left the house. And as soon as they were a few strokes away from the house, Brynn sat down and began to cry. She cried for a long time. Tully stayed by her side, his head in her lap.

After a while, Brynn sniffled and patted Tully on the head. "Things were already bad, Tully," she said. "Why do I always find some way to make them worse? I don't know why I keep saying these things. What am I going to do?"

Tully's eyes looked extra sad, as though he wished to help but couldn't.

Brynn did the only thing she could think of to do —she swam toward the kelp forest. She felt helpless and humiliated, and she cried all the way there. As she approached, she saw the tall strands of kelp waving peacefully, but it didn't make her feel any better. Then, all at once, she saw the dagon she'd seen the other day. The one the sea witch had called Ian. He swam toward Brynn and Tully.

"Why, hello again, little mermaid," he said. "What is all this whimpering and weeping? I could hear you from practically the other side of the ocean."

Brynn wiped at her nose, trying to decide how to

respond.

Ian smiled his sharp-toothed smile. It didn't seem friendly. He swam a little closer.

"Nothing's wrong," said Brynn, still sniffing. "And it's none of your business, anyway."

"Hmm," said Ian. "I wonder. Could it be that the little mermaid still can't do any magic?"

"No," said Brynn.

Ian shrugged. "Oh. That's too bad. Because I thought of something that could help. But if you don't need any help, then I guess you don't care. And, as you say, it's none of my business."

He turned and began swimming away.

"Wait," called Brynn, swimming after him. "Are you serious? You can really help?"

"I thought you didn't need help?"

"Well, if I did, which I'm not saying I do, but if I did, what could you do?"

Ian's sharp teeth showed in his toothy smile again, and from a pocket in his vest, he produced a strand of what looked like jewelry. It was a necklace, with a large, ruby-colored stone attached to a golden chain. Ian let the necklace hang from his scaly, webbed finger for a moment. Then he turned it so that the facets of the ruby caught the light. It flashed and shimmered. Brynn stared at it. It was beautiful, with a strange aspect that made it seem as though it must have been manufactured by some ancient or faraway civilization. But Brynn thought there was something more to it than just beauty and strange craftsmanship. She felt herself staring deeply into the depths of the dark red stone. Was it hypnotizing her? Was she falling under a spell? Brynn shook her head, waggled her tail, and swam back a little way from Ian.

"What is that?" asked Brynn.

"This is a talisman from Lostland."

"Lostland? There's no such place. It's just a myth."

Ian shrugged and went to put the talisman back into his pocket. "If you say so," he muttered.

"Well, hold on," Brynn hastily added. "Tell me more."

Ian grinned slyly and said, "Lostland is real. Or, better to say it *was* real. It was a magical place. Much more magical than this land of merfolk. And you happen to be a very lucky little mermaid because I might just be persuaded to let you borrow this talisman."

"Could it help me do magic?"

"Help you? It can do more than *help* you, mermaid. The person who wears this talisman would be able to cast spells superbly. Yes, it would help you, mermaid. It'd help you be better at magic than anyone in the school—better than your teacher, better than any old mer-magician."

Brynn stared at the talisman. It shimmered

provocatively, but Brynn was suspicious. "Prove it," said Brynn.

The dagon chuckled and slipped the chain over his scaly neck. "Watch," he said. He turned to face the wall of kelp. Then he held out his webbed hands. Instantly, all of the kelp stood straight and still, like soldiers standing at attention. He moved his hands to the right and all the kelp in the forest bent right. He moved it to the left and all the kelp bent left. He waved his hands and the kelp waved in unison with his motion, back and forth, as if every frond of kelp in the forest were some puppet under his control.

Brynn had never seen anything like it. "Wowee," she breathed.

"And that's just a hint of what it can do," said the dagon, scoffing. "With this talisman, you can conjure any of the silly little spells they'll teach you there in that sad little school of yours."

"Like the illumination spell?"

"Nothing to it."

"What about healing spells?"

"Piece of crab cake," said Ian.

He dangled the talisman in front of Brynn again. She reached out to take it, but Ian snatched it away.

"Not so fast," he said. "I'm not just going to let you use it for free. It's going to cost you something."

"But I don't have anything," cried Brynn. "What do you want?"

Ian placed his finger against his fishy lips.

"Hmm," he said as he paced the ocean floor. "Oh, I know. How about your little turtle here?"

"Tully? You want Tully? No, I could never give him up. Why do you want him?"

"Why do you want him?" asked Ian. "A turtle like this could come in handy."

"Well, you can't have him," said Brynn.

"Then you can't have the talisman." Ian pocketed the necklace and pushed off the seafloor. "Let me know if you change your mind," he said as he swam away.

For one brief moment, Brynn had thought her problems would be solved, but now she was back to where she'd been before—everything was hopeless. Brynn sighed and crouched next to Tully, looking into his eyes. She gave him a squeeze.

"It's okay, boy," she said. "Let's go home."

CHAPTER SEVEN

*L*ater that week, during magic class, Windy stopped at Brynn's desk.

"Brynn," said Windy, "why aren't you practicing the lesson?"

Brynn's mouth twisted as she groped for a plausible response. "Well, Mrs. Meyers, it's just I'm not feeling very well today."

This actually wasn't a lie. In fact, Brynn hadn't been feeling very well at all lately. She had lots of stomachaches and headaches, and her muscles felt tight all the time. She was certain it was from the stress of the magic class, but she just didn't know what to do about it.

"Do you need to call home?" asked Mrs. Meyers.

"No," said Brynn. "If I could just sit here and watch, I think I will be fine."

"Okay, if you're sure."

As Mrs. Meyers swam down the other rows, Will leaned across the aisle between the desks.

"You're faking it," he whispered.

"Am not," hissed Brynn.

"Will? Brynn?" said Mrs. Meyers. "Is there a problem over there?"

"No. No problem, Mrs. Myers," said William.

"Let's keep it down, then," said Mrs. Meyers. "Concentrate on your work."

Will sat right next to Brynn, and she knew that he'd probably figured out that she was struggling in the class. He probably even knew that Brynn couldn't conjure a single spell.

"Okay," Mrs. Myers said. "Before we leave for the day, let's talk about ways to power up our magic spells to make them stronger. There are several ways of doing amplification spells. Who can share some?"

Brynn had listened and studied enough to know the answers—spells could be enhanced and enlarged and extended in lots of ways. Singing made spells more powerful, for example. Friendship also helped —two friends casting the same spell together could enlarge their magic so that it added up to more magic than they could conjure separately. Enchanted items, Brynn had recently learned, could also be used to amplify mer-magic. Unfortunately, Brynn didn't know how or why this actually worked because she couldn't cast a single spell yet, so she didn't raise her hand to answer. What was the point of knowing about magic if you couldn't actually *do* magic?

On the speed-current, while Brynn was riding home with Jade, Will swam past Jade and Brynn on his way to take a seat. As he did so, he shot a snide grin in Brynn's direction.

"What's your problem, William Beach?" said Jade with a hard edge in her voice.

"Who, me?" said Will, faking innocence. "Nothing. I guess I was just wondering if Brynn still thinks magic is so super simple—when she can't cast a single spell."

Jade's eyes darted to Brynn. "What's he talking about?"

Brynn shrugged sheepishly, wanting the whole situation to go away.

"Go sit down, William," said Jade. "Brynn can probably do magic better than you and me put together."

"Oh yeah?" said Will, swimming closer. "Really? Have you ever *seen* her do magic?"

"No," spat Jade, "but what difference does that make? I've never seen you pick your nose, but I bet you do it all the time. Besides, who swims around outside class doing magic? Or geometry? Or chemistry?" asked Jade.

Jade really is a loyal friend, even when she's wrong, Brynn thought.

"Of course Brynn can do magic," Jade added.

"Right, Brynn?"

"Uh, yeah, sure," said Brynn. She felt her cheeks getting warm.

"Okay then," said Will to Brynn, "show us."

"She doesn't need to prove anything to you," scoffed Jade.

"You mean she *can't* prove anything," said Will.

"I'm just not feeling very well today," Brynn explained. "I can do a lot more magic than you can, Will."

"Wanna bet on it?"

"Bet on it?" asked Brynn. "What do you mean?"

By now, there were several students around them, crowding in to hear what the fuss was about. Will looked around at them and spoke louder.

"If you're so good at magic," he said, more to the crowd than to Brynn, "you ought to do pretty well on the midterm exam."

Jade laughed. "Well, I know she'll cast mer-magical circles around *you*, William. She'll probably score higher than any of us."

Brynn really did appreciate having a friend to stand up for her, but inwardly she cringed. She needed to downplay this somehow.

"Really?" said Will. "She can get the top score in the class? Okay, how about this for a bet: if Brynn gets the highest grade in our class, I will give her my entire allowance for the month. That's twenty sand dollars. But if she doesn't—" he looked around at the students surrounding them "—if she doesn't, Brynn has to swim *to the bottom of the Craggy Deep.*"

The other students gasped.

The Craggy Deep was a long, deep trench not far from Fulgent. It was a giant crack in the ocean floor that was said to extend all the way to the earth's core. Looking over its edge was like floating on the edge of outer space—not even sunlight could reach the bottom. And it wasn't just the darkness that was scary. For one thing, it was said to be haunted, though haunted by what no one seemed to know. Also, because the water was so cold and dense and heavy, there was less oxygen down there, which made it hard to breathe. No one even knew how deep the Craggy Deep really was, and no one knew what lurked in its depths. Brynn had always been afraid of the place, and her parents told her never to go near it. Goosebumps rose on her arms as she thought about it.

"A whole month's allowance?" marveled Jade. "Pssh. She'll do it. Better be ready to pay up, William."

"Jade!" hissed Brynn.

"It's a bet," said Will.

He held out his hand for Brynn to shake on it, and Brynn couldn't stop herself. She took Will's hand and shook it.

"You saw it, everyone," Will exclaimed. "It's a bet. See you later, Brynn. This is my stop." Will flashed them a snarky grin. He hopped off the speed-current and the crowd that had gathered around dispersed, humming with excitement.

"Jade! Why did you say all those things?"

Jade looked at Brynn and tilted her head. "Everyone was watching, Brynn. I didn't want them to think you were a chicken of the sea."

"But what about the Craggy Deep?" moaned Brynn.

"Pssh," said Jade. "What about it?"

"Well, I've heard it's bottomless, and that there are monsters down there, and it's haunted."

"Omigosh, yes," Jade answered. "It totally is. There are elder sea monsters and sea-ghosts and no-one-knows-what down there. You should never go near it."

Brynn moaned again.

"But you'll never have to," Jade continued. "You really are the best at magic in the whole school—maybe even the whole school district. Aren't you?"

Brynn had gotten herself into this mess. She hadn't meant to, and it had taken a number of steps and missteps, but here she was. Not only was she ready to flunk midterms but she was going to lose this humiliating bet. But how could she possibly admit all of this to her best friend, especially when Jade thought so highly of her? Brynn didn't want to be left behind, and she really didn't want Jade to stop being her friend. That was her main worry. Brynn couldn't shake the idea that if Jade knew how poorly she was doing at magic, that she wouldn't want to be friends anymore.

"Well, I don't know, Jade. Who really cares about who's the best? For all you know, I'm the worst in the whole school," said Brynn.

"Eh," said Jade with a wave of her hand. "Just do a little extra studying. Shouldn't be too hard, and you're going to get twenty sand dollars out of this. That's a lot—you can take us out for clamburgers and kelpshakes."

By the time Brynn got home, she was feeling very sick. Over the next few days, she told her parents she was too sick to even go to school, and this wasn't a lie. But the longer she was away from school, the better Brynn felt. Her stomach stopped hurting, and she started having fun again. In fact, she and Tully were having a game of tag when her parents came home from work.

"Well, someone looks like she's feeling better," said Brynn's mom. She sounded relieved. "Think you can go back to school tomorrow?"

Brynn's face fell. "No, Mom, I can't go back to school."

"Why not, Brynn? You're obviously not sick anymore. Why don't you want to go to school?"

But Brynn didn't have a reason. Not a good reason, anyhow, and not a reason that wouldn't reveal her terrible secrets.

"Please, Mom. Don't make me go," said Brynn.

"Is something at school bothering you, Brynn? Are you being bullied?"

"No, Mom, it's not that, it's just—" For a fleeting moment, Brynn thought about telling her mother, but by now she had told so many lies. She wouldn't just be in trouble for being behind in class, she'd be in trouble for the lies, too.

"It's just what?" asked her mother. Her voice had an edge in it that showed she was running out of patience.

Practicing on her own hadn't worked, and she didn't feel she could ask for help now that it had been so long and she had told so many lies. Everything felt like it was piling up on her and the midterm exams were just two weeks away. The class had learned almost ten different spells now, but Brynn couldn't do any of them. She'd fail the test for sure, which would be bad enough, but now it meant she'd also have to swim in the Craggy Deep or be labeled as the lying mermaid for the rest of her school career.

Brynn glanced at Tully. "Never mind. You're right, Mom. I should get back to school. I don't want to fall behind."

Dana's face softened. "You know you can always tell me if there's something bothering you, right?"

"Sure, Mom. Can I take Tully out for his walk now?"

Her mom brushed a piece of Brynn's hair out from in front of her eyes. "Of course, sweetie. But really, your dad and I are here for you, okay?"

"Yep," said Brynn as she darted for the door.

Outside, she said to Tully, "She says I can tell her anything, but it's better if I can fix this on my own. Come on, Tully. We need to find Ian Fletcher."

CHAPTER EIGHT

*B*rynn's heart pounded as she swam to the speed-current stop. Tully floated along happily at her side, as always. In the late afternoon, there weren't many kids on the speed-current. Instead, it was mostly tired-looking grown-ups, mermen and mermaids on their way home from work.

When Brynn spotted an opening, she looked down at Tully and said, "Come on, Tully, let's go."

They joined the other passengers on the fast-moving speed-current. Brynn found a place to sit, and Tully curled up by her tailfin. Brynn had made up her mind that she was going to find Ian, the dagon who had offered her the Lostland talisman. She couldn't keep up the lies anymore, and she was tired of being the only one in class who couldn't do a magic spell. Something had to give.

Most of the dagons lived in Great Reef. Brynn had never been there before, but she knew it was far from Fulgent, and she'd have to ride the speed-current almost to the very end. She wondered what her parents would think about her going to Great Reef all by herself. She decided they probably wouldn't like it, so she tried not to think about that. This was already difficult enough for Brynn—going to find Ian to tell him she needed his help. Brynn justified it all by telling herself she was doing it for her parents and for the sea itself—wasn't it her responsibility to learn magic and become a sea guardian? She'd let her family down, and it was time to make things right.

Passengers filed on and off the speed-current until almost all of the passengers remaining were dagons. The water in and around the speed-current grew deeper and darker. When the floating sign above the speed-current indicated they had reached Great Reef, Brynn swallowed hard and made her way into the city. Tully swam along by her side, his head swiveled around curiously, and he stopped and sniffed at every sea-shrub lamppost.

Not as much sunlight reached Great Reef, and since the dagons didn't use much magic, the light was provided by luminous plants and little phosphorescent jellyfish in small jars. The place seemed dim to Brynn. Without all the sunlight, there weren't the colorful sea plants and pink and orange coral that Brynn often saw around Fulgent. Instead, there were deeper colors, like dark purple and deep red. Also missing were the colorful fish. Instead, there were gray eels and shadowy fish that darted here and there. It was the first time that Brynn really thought how lucky she was to have the bright colors that were in the fish and plants around her home in Fulgent. She was accustomed to seeing bright blues, yellows, greens, oranges, purples, and pinks everywhere she looked. But in Great Reef, everything was cast in deeper, more dramatic shades.

"I guess they like it this way," Brynn muttered to Tully. "But it makes me a little scared."

Tully looked up at her as if he felt the same way.

The speed-current had brought Brynn to what looked like the middle of town, where there were restaurants, shops, and tall buildings. As Brynn swam down the sidewalk, dagons looked at her curiously. She was one of the only merpeople in sight, and apparently, it wasn't often that a lone little mermaid was seen swimming through downtown Great Reef. Brynn felt a little frightened and lonely, but she had a thought: was this how the dagons felt in Fulgent, her hometown?

A dagon who'd been leaning against a wall pushed off and swam toward her. Brynn's muscles stiffened, and she thought that the stranger may have been coming to hurt her, but he just swam past, and Brynn felt silly for having been frightened. But as she made her way through town, she began to wonder if she could find her way back to the speed-current stop. She had gotten turned around and wasn't sure which direction she was going. Suddenly, she wanted to go back to Fulgent where she felt comfortable and knew the area well, but she was determined to find Ian.

Brynn saw an old dagon woman carrying her groceries along the sidewalk.

Brynn swam up to her. "Excuse me," Brynn said in a very tiny voice. "Do you know where I can find Ian Fletcher?"

"What's that?" the woman barked. "Speak up, I'm old and can't hear you."

Brynn shrank back. "Ian Fletcher?" she repeated.

The woman shook her head and kept on swimming, and so Brynn drifted away.

Brynn was at least grateful to have Tully with her. She knew the sea turtle would try to protect her if she got in trouble. He might not be a very fierce defender, but it was good to have him as company, anyhow. And so Brynn wandered around Great Reef, hoping that she would somehow run into Ian Fletcher. Soon she came to a place where many tall apartment buildings stood. The houses were surrounded by fences, and many of them had sharks in their front yards, secured with chains. As Brynn swam by, the sharks would bang against the fences and scare Brynn, making her swim even faster.

Just when Brynn was ready to give up and take

the speed-current back home, she saw some dagon children playing hopscotch in the street. She swam over to them.

"Could you guys help me?" Brynn asked. "I'm trying to find Ian Fletcher."

The children stared at her without answering.

"D-d-did you hear me?" Brynn stammered. "I'm looking for Ian Fletcher."

"You're not from around here," said a young dagon boy matter-of-factly.

"Um, no, I'm not," said Brynn.

There was a long silence. Brynn waved her tail uncomfortably. Finally, one of the children pointed to a rock house down the street.

"That one," the kid said. "That's where Ian Fletcher lives."

"Thank you," said Brynn as she sighed in relief, but the kids had already started their game back up, and she wasn't sure any of them heard her. She swam away.

When Brynn reached the house, she saw that there was a shark chained up nearby. At first, Brynn hesitated, but then she realized that, even though the shark was swimming in a circle, it was asleep—sharks keep swimming even while asleep. Brynn turned to Tully, placed her finger to her lips, and swam quietly to the door.

She knocked. It was more of a tap.

No answer.

Keeping an eye on the shark, she tapped again.

No answer.

Brynn tapped a third time, but a little harder now.

The door swung open, waking the shark, who sprang into a frenzy of movement and thrashing teeth.

Brynn gasped and fluttered backward.

"Oh, quiet down," Ian Fletcher yelled at the shark. Then, he turned his attention to Brynn. "Don't worry—he's all bark and no bite."

"Do you remember me?" asked Brynn.

"Of course," said Ian. "Of course I remember you."

"I need to speak to you," said Brynn, then leaned closer and whispered, "about that magic talisman."

Ian looked around outside, checking to see if anyone was watching. "Okay," he said. "Come on in."

It was very dark inside Ian's house. Brynn bumped into a table. Tully stayed close. She bumped into a lamp.

"Sorry," said Brynn. "It's kinda dark in here."

"Well, I don't need lots of bright magic and pretty lights to find my way around."

"That's what I wanted to talk to you about," said Brynn. "I want the talisman from Lostland. I can pay you for it. I have fifteen sand dollars now that I've saved from my allowance, and I'll be getting another twenty after midterms from a bet I've made."

"Money?" Ian exclaimed. "I don't want money."

"Well, I could do some magic for you then," said Brynn. "Bring some light in here, for example."

"I already have the talisman," said Ian. "If I wanted magic, I could do it myself."

"Well, that's all I've got. Please, Ian, I need it. What can I give you?"

"I already told you, little mermaid, I'll give you the talisman when you give me your turtle."

"No," said Brynn. "I can't give you Tully. No way."

"Then I guess we don't have a deal." Ian opened his front door and motioned for Brynn to leave.

But Brynn didn't move. She was thinking about the bet she'd made and the Craggy Deep, and she was thinking of her parents' and teacher's disappointment. But most of all, Brynn was thinking that the purpose of a mermaid was to protect the ocean, and the mermaids did that through mer-magic. If she couldn't even do mer-magic, then what was she even good for?

She loved Tully, and she didn't want to give him up, but Brynn couldn't see any other option.

"Okay," she said sadly. "I'll do it."

"Great," said Ian flatly. "Hand him over."

"What do you want with him?" Brynn asked.

"None of your business," said Ian.

"You won't hurt him, will you?"

"No," said Ian. "I'm not going to hurt your little pet."

Brynn knelt down beside Tully and wrapped her arms around his neck. "I'm sorry, boy," she said as she began to cry. "Maybe I can come and visit sometime."

When she looked up, Ian held the talisman out to her. Brynn grabbed it.

"Now, don't let your teacher look too closely at that," said Ian. "From what I've heard, merfolk using talismans in school is considered cheating."

Brynn knew this, of course, and under ordinary circumstances, she would never even try to cheat or give away her pet turtle. But things had gotten so desperate, so hopeless. Brynn was out of options and out of time.

"Well, thanks," said Brynn gloomily as she shoved the necklace in her backpack.

"Bye-bye, little mermaid," said the dagon. "It was a pleasure doing business with you."

It had gotten quite late by the time Brynn rode the speed-current home. As she walked into her home, both her parents were waiting for her.

"Brynn, where have you been?" her mother questioned.

"And where's Tully?" her father asked.

Very quickly, a lie formed in Brynn's mind.

"Oh, Mom, Dad. Tully ran away." It hurt Brynn to say the words. "I've been looking for him all day.

He's nowhere to be found." She began to cry—this part wasn't fake.

"Oh, Brynn," said her father. "I'm so sorry. Sometimes turtles go off like that. We'll look for him tomorrow, but it could be he was just ready to move on."

And just like that, Brynn had not only gotten the talisman, she had escaped punishment for being out late. As she fell fitfully to sleep that night, Brynn couldn't help but notice the empty place at the end of her bed where Tully slept, and it gave her the saddest feeling. To distract herself from thinking of him, Brynn took the talisman from her backpack and stared into its deep red glowing depths. Tomorrow she'd be able to do magic. Perhaps there was even a spell to recover pet turtles. Tomorrow everything would be different.

CHAPTER NINE

The next morning, Brynn left the house and swam toward the speed-current stop before she took the Lostland talisman from her backpack. No one could find out she had the talisman. No one could find out what it was for. Not Jade or Will or her parents, and certainly not Mrs. Windy Meyers.

Brynn told herself that she did not plan to keep the magical artifact for very long. She didn't want to cheat her way through learning magic, even though she had the feeling that she would be able to cast some very powerful mer-magic by using the talisman. But that wasn't the point, she repeated to herself. She would be a great mer-magician without the talisman. Brynn reasoned that she needed the talisman only to catch up in school and to maybe figure out a way to get Tully back. Then she'd get rid of it. She'd bury it, or toss it into the Craggy Deep, maybe. Or she might take it to the surface and leave it—humans were always looking for treasure from the ocean.

And so, just before the speed-current stop came into her view, Brynn checked behind her and up and down the street. She looked up above her, and then she checked all around her all over again. Then Brynn slipped the chain over her head and around her neck. The red jewel hung there sparkling. It was, in fact, quite beautiful, though Brynn reminded herself that she'd need to tuck it into her jacket to conceal it. The red jewel sparkled and flashed in the morning sun. Brynn was sure it was warming her, and she felt something else coming from the necklace —but what was it? What was she feeling?

In any case, Brynn liked the Lostland talisman. Not just because it was nice looking, but because it was her key to getting out of the various messes she'd gotten herself into lately. But what else was it that she felt?

Power.

That was it—the talisman made her feel powerful, and this gave her the impression that she was in control. She felt confident with the Lostland talisman around her neck, and she knew that confidence was an important part of conjuring magic and casting spells. No wonder the talisman was good at amplifying magic.

"But I will not keep it," Brynn muttered to herself.

"It's just to get me caught up and get Tully back and show everyone how good at magic I am."

Brynn hadn't gotten a chance to test out the magic with the talisman. She'd been too afraid someone would spot her or ask about the talisman. And she wouldn't have any chance to test the talisman between here and school, either. As she made her way to the speed-current stop, she saw Jade waiting for her.

"Nice necklace," said Jade as Brynn swam up. "Where'd ya get it?"

"Oh, this old thing? I dunno. It was a gift or something."

"It's so pretty," said Jade as they boarded the speed-current.

Brynn buttoned her jacket and then furtively tucked the jewel in so that it wouldn't attract too much attention.

Once again, as they rode to school, Brynn found herself having a hard time concentrating. Now, however, instead of feeling worry and guilt and pressure, she felt excitement. Okay, she maybe still felt the guilt, and she wondered if Ian would take care of Tully and make sure he went to the surface, but mostly, she really could not wait to go to magic class.

Her day passed at the lazy, slow pace of a basking shark. Brynn swam from class to class in a daze. She stared at her lunch without taking a nibble. She could think of nothing but magic class.

At last, it was time. As she swam swiftly toward the classroom, Brynn squeezed the talisman in her hand.

"Please work," she whispered. "Please work, please work, please work."

Windy took her place at the front of the class.

"All right, everyone, listen up," she said. "Midterms are tomorrow. It's time to practice the things that we've been studying so far and make sure that you're ready for the test. I want you to partner up with the person sitting next to you and practice all of the magic skills you've been taught."

Brynn looked to her right. Will looked back and grinned at her.

"I guess we're partners," he said. "Now we'll see if you can do any magic."

"Don't worry about me," said Brynn. "Worry about yourself. Jade and I are going for clamburgers and kelpshakes after you hand over that allowance."

That shut Will up for a moment—perhaps Brynn's confidence had made him believe she really did know magic. But then he quickly conjured a simple light spell, holding up his index finger from which a small flame glowed like a candle.

"Eh, not bad," Brynn said, acting very bored. "But watch this."

Now was the moment Brynn would discover if her plan would work or if she would simply sink deeper into trouble and despair. She hadn't tested the talisman and she had yet to cast a single effective spell. She'd seen Ian Fletcher do a few very impressive tricks with the talisman, but he could have tricked her. What if the talisman was just some old hunk of shiny glass?

Brynn took a deep breath.

Will folded his arms and raised one eyebrow.

Brynn began making the motions that she'd seen Mrs. Meyers and the rest of the class making all week to cast illumination spells. She'd never really tried it for real—before she got the talisman, she was still working on mastering the basic energy sphere.

But when she crossed her hands in front of herself, and then raised one hand, instead of a single small flame no brighter than a match, like Will's, a brilliant flame even bigger than her hand leaped to life, casting a nearly blindingly bright light through the entire class. All heads in the class turned to see. Will squinted and held up a hand to the dazzling flame.

The other students gasped and pointed.

"Whoa," said Will.

Windy was on the other side of the room helping other students, but the spell had captured her notice. Her mouth fell open.

"Well done, Brynn!" she cried.

Brynn smiled with pure delight. It was working!

Will blinked and rubbed his eyes, half-blinded by

Brynn's spell. He eyed her curiously. "How—how'd you do that?"

Brynn shrugged and said, "Toldja—mer-magic comes easily to me."

He narrowed his eyes, but then they got back to work, practicing together. For every spell that Will cast, Brynn cast one that was much stronger and a lot more impressive.

By the end of class, Will pressed his lips together and shrugged his shoulders. With a reluctant look on his face, he said, "Well, I gotta tell ya, Brynn: I was wrong about you. You can really cast a spell!"

Brynn felt the talisman growing hot against her skin. The red jewel glowed beneath the fabric of her jacket, and for a brief moment, it felt like some of that hot redness seeped into Brynn's mind.

"That's because you're a big ugly dummy," she replied.

She instantly clapped her hands over her mouth. Why had she said that? Even if Will did bother her sometimes, Brynn didn't think he was a big ugly dummy. He was a nice-looking boy, and could be quite kind at times. Most times, in fact. He'd been trying to be kind just then, so why had she made such an unkind remark?

Will's eyes dropped to the floor. He drifted back to his desk without saying anymore.

"Will," Brynn said. "I'm sorry. I didn't mean it."

But Will wouldn't look over at her now. "That's all right," he mumbled. "I'll just leave you alone."

As soon as the school bell rang, Will grabbed his backpack and dashed out of the classroom. Brynn tried to catch up with him. She wanted to explain that she didn't think he was dumb or ugly, and he wasn't particularly big for that matter. She wanted to let him know that she thought he was a really nice merboy, and that she didn't know why she'd been mean to him. But it was the end of the school day and hundreds of mer-kids were swimming through the corridors and out of the doors. Brynn lost Will in the crowd.

Jade met Brynn at the speed-current stop to go home.

"Brynn!" cried Jade. "I heard from Lyndi Mariana about what happened in magic class! Have you been practicing? Are you going to ace the midterm? What did Will say? Are you really the best in class? Tell me! Tell me!" said Jade.

The talisman glowed again. It grew warm under Brynn's jacket. Brynn felt a sort of hot irritation inside her, mixed with a heavy, almost smothering sense of pride.

"Yeah," she said haughtily, "I'm sure they're all talking. Sometimes I feel like I'm the only interesting mer-kid in this whole pathetic school." And she again gasped and clapped a hand over her mouth. What was wrong with her?

"Rude," said Jade, giving a Brynn perplexed look. "Gee, stuck-up much, Brynn?"

Before she could stop herself, Brynn heard herself saying, "Yeah, maybe. And if you don't like it, there are lots of mer-friends in the sea you can hang out with."

Jade's mouth fell open in total shock. She looked as though she might say something back, but then she simply drifted away from Brynn without looking back. Then Jade hopped on the speed-current.

"Jade, wait!" hollered Brynn. She jumped into the speed-current, too, but the speed-current was packed with after-school riders and Brynn couldn't find Jade.

What was happening? Brynn didn't understand. It felt like the words were just flying out of her mouth, as though someone or something else was controlling her.

Just then, two nearby students were goofing off with each other, throwing a football around as they sat on the speed-current. One of them overthrew the ball and it bonked Brynn on the head.

The boys looked at her, obviously embarrassed.

"Sorry!" said one of them. "You okay?"

"Yeah, my bad," said the merboy who'd thrown the ball. "Sorry."

The talisman burned against Brynn's skin, and she was filled with hot anger.

"You clumsy oafs!" Brynn yelled. "How dumb do

you have to be to think it's okay to throw a ball around on a crowded speed-current?"

The merboys sank back away from her.

"Sorry," muttered one of them again.

This isn't me, thought Brynn. *I don't like this.*

But she didn't know how to quell the anger inside her. She pointed a finger at the ball. A tight beam of mer-magic sprang from her fingertip, there was a bright flash, and an instant later, the football was just a cloud of vapor.

The boys and other speed-current riders looked on, astonished and appalled. Brynn grabbed her backpack and jumped off the speed-current. The talisman throbbed and flashed with something like satisfaction, and Brynn knew it was the talisman that was making her act this way. She hurriedly removed it, and the angry red light drained from the jewel.

Brynn never wanted to wear the talisman ever again. As she held the artifact in her hand, she felt like she should swim straight to the Craggy Deep and hurl it into the blackness.

But then she paused.

The mer-magic midterm was tomorrow. Without the talisman, she couldn't do any spells at all, let alone pass a magic test. She wouldn't be able to do a single spell on the exam and that meant she'd fail—she'd fail spectacularly. Mrs. Meyers would be disappointed. Her parents would be angry. The other students would make fun of her. She'd lose the bet with Will. She'd have to swim in the Craggy Deep. It would be awful. It would be the worst thing that ever happened to her. At least, that's what Brynn told herself.

Besides, hadn't she given up Tully for this? Could it really hurt to just wear it one more time? She'd just wear it for the midterm exam, find Ian, and get Tully back, and then she wouldn't wear it ever again. Brynn buried the talisman in her backpack and swam all the way home, thinking about Jade. What could she do to make things right again?

She had to tell Jade.

Yes, that was the only solution. She had hurt Jade's feelings too much to just apologize. And they were best friends. She would tell Jade about her struggles with magic and the dagon and the talisman and everything. Jade would understand, wouldn't she?

But Brynn couldn't tell her quite yet. Brynn couldn't tell anyone until she passed her midterm exam. Brynn relaxed a little and swam for home, and she even smiled a little because she knew she wasn't just going to *pass* the midterm, she was going to get the highest grade in the class.

Maybe the highest score in the whole school.

No, she would get the highest score in all of mer-history.

CHAPTER TEN

The day of the midterm exams had arrived. Brynn woke up feeling so nervous that she could barely breathe. She hastily made her bed and got dressed, and then she peeked inside her backpack for the tenth time to make sure the Lostland talisman was still there. Brynn didn't dare put it on now. If it made her speak rudely or act rashly, her parents might suspect something was wrong. Instead, she kept it buried under her books.

She was almost out the door when her father said, "Brynn? Are you going to eat breakfast?"

"No! Not today!"

He poked his head out from the kitchen. "What's the matter, kiddo? Nervous about midterms?"

"You have no idea," she replied.

Adrian smiled at her. "Ahh, well, a little nervousness is okay. But if you've studied hard, all you can do is your best."

Brynn nodded, feeling her face flush with guilt.

Brynn's mom joined her father in the kitchen. "Good luck on your tests today, sweetie!"

"Thanks," said Brynn, rushing for the door. "Bye!"

As she swam to the speed-current stop, Brynn tried to think of what she would say to Jade. She promised herself she'd eventually explain the whole sorry mess to Jade after midterms.

But for now, she could say something like, "Oh, Jade, I'm so sorry. I've been under so much stress, and I lost my pet turtle. Please, please forgive me!"

She practiced as she approached the speed-current stop.

Or maybe, Brynn thought, she should downplay the whole thing and say something more like, "Ah, lighten up, Jade. I was only kidding around. C'mon, don't be so serious!"

Brynn practiced this approach a few times.

In the end, it didn't matter because Jade wasn't at the speed-current stop, and she didn't show up even after Brynn waited until she was very late for first period. Jade had gone on to school without Brynn. For seven years, she and Jade had walked to school together, and now, on maybe the most important day of her whole school career, Brynn would have to get to school by herself.

Brynn fought back her tears, wishing she could go back in time and try harder in Windy's magic class. In fact, if she were going to travel back in time, Brynn wished she could go back to fifth grade, when she had recess with her best friend and long lunches and no magic class!

She hopped on the speed-current. There were a few other late students nearby. To Brynn's surprise, they drifted a little way off when they saw Brynn, as though they didn't want to be too close to her. Brynn noticed and felt her cheeks turning red. The other kids didn't want to be around her. She tried to pretend she didn't notice, but it seemed so obvious. No mer-student was anywhere close to her.

She lifted her head and tried to make her face look like she didn't care.

At least I'm going to ace the midterms, Brynn thought. *Most of these dum-dums won't even be able to pass.*

Why was she thinking such awful things? Was the talisman affecting her even when she wasn't wearing it?

When lunchtime arrived, Brynn saw Jade sitting at their usual spot. Brynn swam up with her lunch tray, but before she sat down, Jade stood up to go.

"Jade!" Brynn said. "Don't go. I want to talk to you. I'm sorry, please."

"Not now, Brynn," said Jade. "I've got midterms

today, too, and I don't want you making me any more upset than you already have."

With Jade and the other students treating her coldly, Brynn didn't even feel like eating. How long had it been since she'd really enjoyed a seanut butter and jellyfish sandwich?

Brynn wished she could talk to someone about her problems. She wished she could talk to anyone. She wanted to talk to her mom, but that would only get her in trouble. Even more than talking with her mom, Brynn wished she could talk to Tully and cuddle with him. Tully never judged her for anything she did. She could tell the little turtle anything. And if she were better at magic, maybe she'd even be able to speak to and understand him someday.

But the likelihood of that happening seemed almost impossible. Tully was gone, and she'd never be able to do magic. Not really. A deep sadness fell over Brynn. She felt as though an anchor were tied around her neck.

When sixth period arrived, Brynn reached into her bag and retrieved the talisman. She strung it around her neck, and the jewel throbbed and glittered against her chest. Brynn decided that if the talisman made her say mean things, then she would just not say anything to anyone. She kept her mouth clamped shut and avoided even looking at the other mer-students.

The tests for magical ability were completed by

performing spells in front of a proctor, a merperson who observed the exams and marked down scores. Windy asked the students to read silently until they were called to go see the proctor in another room for their examination. They would take the test one by one, with only the proctor. Brynn was especially grateful that Windy had told them to read silently.

At last, Brynn was called to go before the proctor. She went down the corridor according to Windy's instructions and entered a small room. Inside sat an old but friendly looking merman with thick eyeglasses. His head was bare, but from his chin grew the long, gray beard of a scholar. His tail was gray and encrusted with barnacles. He sat at a desk, and he held a clipboard. Across from him, there stood an empty chair.

"Brynn Finley?" asked the proctor, tilting his head and looking down at his clipboard.

Brynn kept her mouth clamped shut and only nodded emphatically in reply.

"How are you feeling today?"

Afraid that she would say something awful, Brynn didn't answer. Instead, she nodded again.

The proctor chuckled. "A bit nervous, eh? That's natural. Very well. Take a seat and let's get on with it."

The merman gestured at the chair and Brynn sat down, still keeping her mouth shut tight.

"Brynn Finley," said the proctor, "please demonstrate the basic energy sphere."

With the talisman around her neck and buried in her jacket, Brynn effortlessly and quickly conjured a perfect little energy sphere. It shone hotly and with a tinge of red, perfectly round and steady.

The proctor raised his eyebrows and nodded his approval before making some marks on the paper held in his clipboard. "Excellent," he muttered, mostly to himself. "Very good."

The proctor then asked Brynn to cast the basic illumination spell. She did so without so much as taking a breath. The proctor held up an arm to the blinding blaze of Brynn's magical flame, but again he nodded approvingly as he jotted down his notes.

It's working, thought Brynn. *I'm going to pass!*

Brynn cast all of her spells the same way—she exerted very little effort and every spell was perfect and curiously powerful. After a few more spells, the proctor removed his glasses and studied Brynn. She sat up straight in the chair and flicked her long, lavender locks from her shoulder. She wore a smug and superior grin on her face.

The proctor folded his glasses and tapped them in the palm of his hand.

"Brynn Finley," he said. "Can you throw me a ball of illumination?"

She did so, quickly and perfectly. The proctor

captured the ball in his gnarly old hand and extinguished it.

"Can you throw me two illumination balls?"

Brynn did it, almost without paying attention to the proctor. The proctor caught them in his hands and put them out.

The proctor now had one eyebrow cocked high, and he was nodding slightly to himself. Was he suspicious?

"Can you throw me *five* balls of magic illumination, Brynn Finley?" he asked.

She conjured five balls of illumination, each precisely the same size but each one a different color —green, blue, golden, white, and the last one was a deep, ruby red, like the talisman of Lostland. She juggled them, just to get her point across, and then shot them across the room at the proctor, who almost could not react fast enough to capture them in his hands. He replaced the glasses on his face and stared at Brynn.

"Your test is complete. Very impressive, Ms. Finley," he said after a long pause. "The results of the test won't be released until next week, but you've done very well."

Brynn smiled, got up from the chair.

"As a matter of fact," said the proctor, frowning down at his clipboard, "I don't recall a student who ever had mer-magic quite as strong as yours."

That means I'll score the highest in the school!

thought Brynn. She wanted to thank the proctor, but she still wasn't sure she could speak without saying something completely and utterly disrespectful, so she just smiled some more and bowed her head and opened the door.

"However," said the proctor, "I have one more question for you."

Uh oh.

"I noticed you are wearing a necklace," he said, swimming out from behind his desk.

Brynn nodded again, but she only waved goodbye and turned to go.

"The chain is of unique craftsmanship," he said. "Very unique. May I see it? Can you tell me where it came from?"

Brynn froze. She wouldn't have been able to answer even if she allowed herself to.

The proctor began swimming closer. "Could you let me see it, please?" He held out his hand.

Brynn slipped her hand into the neck of her jacket and clutched the talisman, her mind racing, unsure what to do. She could swim away, but the show of defiance might invite further suspicion. She could show the proctor the talisman, of course—maybe he wouldn't know that she was using it to amplify her magic and cheat.

But he probably would.

Before Brynn had time to make up her mind, and before the proctor had crossed the room, another student entered the room through the open door.

"Hi," he said. Brynn knew the merboy. His name was Stewie Tide. "Am I too early?" he asked, looking from Brynn to the proctor.

"Erhm, no," stammered the proctor, "that is, Ms. Finley, if I could just—"

Brynn swam off without looking back. She darted into an adjoining corridor and then another. When she thought she was fully out of sight, Brynn let out a heavy sigh. Then she pulled the talisman off and jammed it back in her backpack.

I did it! she thought, and she began making plans to find Ian Fletcher to get Tully back. When the class bell rang, Brynn left feeling more relaxed than she had in a long time. She spotted Jade leaving the building and so she swam fast to catch up with her.

"Jade!" she called, and this time Jade stopped and floated there, waiting.

"What do you want?" Jade asked. Her tone of voice had a certain iciness. She was still angry.

But, Brynn reasoned, the fact that Jade had stopped to wait for her probably meant that, with a proper, sincere apology, she and Jade would be best friends again. With a flick of her tail, Brynn swam more quickly toward Jade.

"Was there something you wanted to tell me," Jade said as Brynn approached.

"Yes! Yes!" said Brynn.

"I thought so," said Jade.

Jade's arms were folded tightly, and she looked quite cross, but even so, Brynn thought she detected the hint of a smile on Jade's lips.

"I wanted to tell you—" began Brynn.

"Yeah?" replied Jade. "Go on."

"I wanted to tell you that I'm pretty sure I can find a better friend than you," said Brynn. Her eyes flew open, trying to understand what she herself was saying, but before she could stop herself, she continued. "And I don't think I ever liked you, anyhow."

It wasn't true! Jade was Brynn's best friend and always had been. Brynn loved Jade!

Brynn clamped both of her hands over her mouth, almost over her whole face, to keep herself from saying anything else. But tears welled up in Jade's eyes—even the ocean couldn't hide them.

"Okay, Brynn. I see how it is. I hope you did well on your exam."

With a dreary wave of her tail, Jade floated away.

Brynn was feeling more agony now than ever. She wasn't even wearing the talisman, so why had she said those things? She didn't mean any of them, not at all, and it tore her up inside to think that Jade thought Brynn might really think those things.

Brynn pulled the talisman out of her bag. The talisman wasn't powered by mer-magic, which meant it wasn't powered by love. It came from some other source. Was it possible that it was some dark magic and that it was rubbing off on her? That would mean that the more she used it, the stronger the effect it had on her? Was it permanent? If she used it too much, would she always be hateful and cruel? If that happened, she'd be an outcast, friendless, alone. Brynn put the talisman back in her bag again.

I have to get rid of it, thought Brynn, *immediately*.

CHAPTER ELEVEN

*I*nstead of riding the speed-current home, Brynn rode straight to Great Reef. She didn't just want to get rid of the talisman; she wanted to see Tully and to bring him home. She missed him so much it hurt. But when Brynn got to Ian's house and knocked on his door, no one answered, even as the shark outside his home snapped and thrashed on his chain. Brynn kept knocking until a young dagon boy in the street called to her.

"Hey, mermaid, Ian's not home," said the boy.

"Do you know where he is?"

"He's at work. He said he was headed for the quarries."

"Did he have a pet turtle with him?"

"He's always got turtles with him. And if he's not home, he's usually at the quarries."

"Thank you!" yelled Brynn and she swam away

immediately. *Turtles?* she thought. *More than one?* And she couldn't imagine why anyone would ever go out to the quarries. It was a vast stretch of desolate ocean. The ocean floor there was sandy and rocky and gravelly—with very little vegetation or coral or life of any kind. Almost no sea creatures dwelled there. As far as Brynn had ever heard, dagons and merfolk went there mostly just to get rocks, boulders, and sand for building projects. The area was large, dark, and desolate, and it was even farther from Brynn's home than Great Reef.

It was so empty, in fact, that once Brynn arrived there, she immediately spotted someone in the distance. Several someones, actually. In the distance, she saw what looked like five or six sea creatures swimming together in a line, one behind the other. She swam closer and realized that the creatures were sea turtles, strung together in a livestock harness. The dagon named Ian Fletcher was behind the turtles. In one hand, he held the reins, and in the other, he brandished a whip! These were work turtles, and together, they pulled against a boulder the size of a washing machine. It was lashed to the harness with ropes made of kelp.

"Yaw!" cried Ian Fletcher, cracking the whip over the heads of the turtles. "Get along! Pull!"

The turtles at the front of the line were large and muscular. They looked to Brynn like they could move a house, but the boulder didn't seem to move at all.

The turtles in the rear of the line were smaller. Then Brynn saw Tully, who was the smallest of them all, straining against the braces. He looked pale, beat-up, and exhausted.

Ian Fletcher cracked the whip over their heads again and the turtles surged forward with their load. Brynn hurriedly swam over to them.

"Pull, pull!" Ian shouted.

"Let my turtle go!" shouted Brynn.

Ian tightened up on the reins and his team of turtles stopped pulling. The boulder hadn't budged.

"What are you doing here?" demanded Ian.

"What are *you* doing?" Brynn shot back.

"I am trying to move this rock," said Ian. "I'm working! This is my job!"

"You can't make Tully move rocks!"

"I think you've forgotten," said Ian. "Tully belongs to me now."

"But you promised you wouldn't hurt him!"

Ian held out his arms and webbed hands. "Oh, I'm not hurting him at all."

He came forward and stood beside the line of turtles, patting them on their backs. They flinched at his touch. Tully shut his eyes and cowered.

"Does it look like these turtles are being harmed?" Ian said gruffly.

"Yes!" cried Brynn. "You're whipping them. They're obviously miserable!"

Ian shrugged. "Well, just because I don't play

fetch with my turtles, or scratch their bellies before they go to bed, that doesn't mean they're being mistreated. I feed them and keep them in a stable at the surface. And this Tully here is a hard little worker. He'll soon make a really great work turtle."

Tully pleaded with his eyes to be set free. He looked frightened and confused. The other turtles looked surly and tired.

"Now," added Ian Fletcher, "if you'll leave me alone, I can get back to work."

Brynn rummaged in her backpack and pulled out the talisman. "The deal's off!" she shouted. "I want Tully back!"

She held the talisman out to Ian, but he merely shook his head.

"Young mermaid," said Ian, growling as though trying to keep from screaming. "That is definitely not how this works. You have the talisman, I have the turtle, and I don't feel like trading."

"Please," said Brynn, "I never should have made the deal in the first place. You can have the talisman back, and I can give you some sand dollars, just please, please give me my turtle back!"

"No, I don't think so," said Ian, exasperated. But then he smiled a smile that was not very warm or friendly. "Not unless you want to take his place."

"Take the talisman," said Brynn. "You can move your rock with magic."

Ian kicked at the rock. "You think I never considered that? This particular rock can't be moved with magic. Now go on home and let me do my job."

Brynn took the talisman in her hand and concentrated on moving the huge heavy rock with her magic. Sparks and bubbles and flashes of light emitted from the water and the talisman and the rock itself, but the rock stayed put.

"See?" said Ian. "Certain things call for good old-fashioned work. You should be going. Up, turtles! Pull!"

The turtles roused themselves and flapped their fins, and the harness tightened. The rock, on the other hand, refused to move.

"No!" yelled Brynn. She dove down to Tully and began undoing the buckles and harness. Ian flicked his whip and it cracked in the water close to Brynn. She jumped back in fear.

Ian moved closer and inspected Tully's harness, pulling the straps tight again.

Brynn scowled and clutched at the talisman again. An energy sphere formed and spun madly. It began to move in Ian Fletcher's direction. His eyes grew wide and he faltered back. The sphere grew, and Ian held out one hand.

I'll hit him with a shock spell or a sleep spell, Brynn thought.

Then, all at once, the talisman sputtered and winked out, dark as any ordinary jewel. Brynn's energy sphere vanished.

"Ah ha!" said Ian, pointing his scaly finger at Brynn. "You've overworked the talisman with all your schoolwork! Not to mention your efforts to bother me! I should tell you that I am on official business for Phaedra the sea witch, and if you don't quit interfering, I'm going to let her know you're interfering. And, trust me—you do not want to be on Phaedra's bad side. No sirree."

Brynn looked at Tully. He was quaking in his harness. The happy colors on his shell had drained, and he wore bruises from the brutal work. Brynn tossed the talisman angrily at Ian and glared at him fiercely.

Ian gazed coolly at Brynn.

Then Brynn darted back to Tully's side again. But before Ian could draw back his whip again, Brynn whispered, "I'll be back," and then she swam away as quickly as she could.

CHAPTER TWELVE

*B*rynn had to tell someone her problems, and there was only one person she trusted enough with the entire wild and terrible tale.

She could have gone to her parents, obviously. They loved Brynn, of course, and would always do whatever they could to help her, but Brynn was too ashamed of revealing her magical failures, giving away Tully to a dagon taskmaster, and all the little lies she'd told. The thought of speaking to her parents made Brynn's face blush and her scales shiver with shame.

Brynn had also considered confessing everything to her magic teacher. Windy Meyers was so helpful, smart, and understanding—she would probably stand by Brynn, too. And Windy might even help smooth things out with Brynn's parents. But Brynn had cheated in Windy's class—how could Windy ever forgive Brynn for that?

This sad little mermaid felt very alone in the immensity of the sea at that moment, but she simply couldn't handle the situation on her own anymore. Brynn needed help, lots of it, and even if there was no one who could help her, she felt that she had to at least tell someone else what had happened, if only to unburden her sore heart.

There was only one person left who might listen.

When Jade answered the front door of her house and saw Brynn floating there on the front porch, she took one look at Brynn and immediately began closing the door again. But Jade was Brynn's best and forever friend. The two mermaids had sworn to each other to always be there for one another. And so Jade closed the door very, very slowly.

"Wait!" Brynn called. "Please, Jade, I'm begging you."

The door paused, but Jade stayed behind it, hidden.

"Jade, I'm so sorry for everything that I've said and done," said Brynn, her eyes looking down on her tail. "I've been such a bad friend. Please just talk to me one more time."

Jade peeked around the edge of the door. "You've really hurt my feelings, Brynn."

Brynn winced and wrung her hands. She tried to imagine what it'd be like to be Jade and to have her best friend say such awful things. Jade had no idea that the talisman had caused Brynn to be so mean. It must have hurt horribly to have thought that Brynn actually meant what she'd said. Friends don't treat each other that way. Brynn knew that, and she knew the talisman had made her say what she did, but she knew that if she hadn't tried to shortcut her way out of her problems, she'd have never put the talisman around her neck. And she knew that if she tried to make excuses for the terrible things she'd said and done, Jade would only close the door the rest of the way.

"I know," said Brynn. "I'm sorry, Jade. Please, can we talk?"

Jade agreed to go for a swim with Brynn, and as they swam, Brynn told her everything. She started with how she wasn't able to do the magic spells and her encounter with Phaedra the sea witch and Ian the dagon. She told her about how everything got worse with Will's dare and how she missed Tully so much.

Jade said nothing but made little amazed noises as they swam along.

By the time they'd reached the kelp forest and Brynn's favorite clearing, Brynn had come to the part about using the talisman to ace the test and how the talisman was incredibly powerful, but it made Brynn say the cruelest and most inappropriate things.

Jade's eyes were wide and her mouth opened in astonishment.

Brynn finally finished her sad tale, coming to the part where Ian had made Tully into a work turtle and was forcing him to pull some big enchanted rock with a team of other turtles.

When she'd gotten the whole story out, Brynn breathed a long sigh of relief. Repeating it all almost brought her to tears, and she realized how hard it'd been to keep it all inside.

Jade didn't speak for what seemed like an hour. All she could do was blink and shake her head.

"Wow, Brynn," said Jade at last. "That's quite a story."

"And I am sorry, Jade," said Brynn. "I am so sorry that I hurt your feelings. Honest. I feel just awful about it. I've let everyone down, including my best friend. You've always been there for me, and I let you down. Can you ever forgive me?"

This last part was hard for Brynn to ask, one of the hardest things she'd ever had to do.

"Yes," Jade said with a small smile. "I forgive you."

The two young mermaids embraced.

"I promise I'll never treat you like that ever again," said Brynn. "You're too good of a person and too good of a friend, and it scares me that I almost ruined our friendship."

"It's okay," said Jade. "I understand. I'll get over it. For now, let's focus on getting Tully back. Let's go tell our parents. If anyone has strong magic, it's our parents. I'm sure they'll help us."

"No," Brynn said sharply. "I mean, no, please. I'll get in so much trouble. Please can we keep this between us? For now?"

Jade's mouth twisted, and Brynn could see plainly that Jade didn't like the idea.

"Please, Jade?" Brynn implored.

Jade sighed. "Fine. What's your plan?"

"I don't have a plan," said Brynn.

Jade began to swim back and forth. She always paced whenever she was thinking deeply. Brynn followed behind her. They swam one direction and then the other across the clearing in the kelp.

"So, you don't have the talisman anymore?" Jade asked, holding her chin in her hand like a detective.

"No," said Brynn gloomily. "It fizzled. I threw it at Ian Fletcher the dagon."

Jade stroked her chin thoughtfully. "And you can't do any magic on Ian Fletcher to make him release Tully?"

"Well, technically, I can't do *any* magic. So, no, I can't do any magic on Ian Fletcher or the rock or on Tully."

Jade seemed to be closely examining the scales that covered her beautiful tail, but Brynn knew she was thinking hard.

"So," said Jade after a few moments, "what about

A.M. LUZZADER

the corral where the work turtles are kept? It's got to be at the surface so that the turtles can breathe. Presumably, Ian Fletcher can't stay there day and night, right?"

"Jade, you're a genius!" said Brynn. She was so glad that she and Jade would be friends again, and now she was even more pleased she'd asked Jade for help.

The two mermaids hurried back to where Brynn had seen Ian and Tully and the other work turtles, but only the huge, apparently enchanted rock remained there. They searched the area high and low, but there was no Ian, no turtles, and no sign of a work-turtle corral.

Brynn began to despair, but Jade kept her spirits up.

"We'll just have to keep looking," said Jade. "Where does this Ian guy live?"

It had gotten dark by the time they reached Ian's apartment building in Great Reef. They swam quietly toward Ian Fletcher's apartment, careful not to upset his watch-shark in the front yard. Jade directed Brynn to some sea-shrubs across the street, and the two of them huddled behind them, watching Ian's building.

"What are we gonna do now?" asked Brynn.

"We're gonna wait," replied Jade.

"For what?"

"Well, for something. I'll let you know when I see it."

"How long will we have to wait? I don't know about you, but my parents are going to call the police soon if I don't show up at home."

"I don't think it will be long," Jade opined. Then she muttered, "At least I hope it's not long—my parents will probably call the cops before yours do."

It just so happened that they waited less than half an hour. Ian Fletcher came floating out of his front door, patted his shark roughly on the head, and then began to swim upward, toward the surface.

"He's going to the surface!" exclaimed Brynn, barely able to keep her voice to a whisper. "To the turtle corral!"

Jade nodded wisely. "That's what I was hoping he'd do."

"Gosh, I should have come to you weeks ago," said Brynn in an amazed voice.

As predicted, Ian swam straight to the surface, near a small sandy island. There, by the beach, was the corral of the work turtles, encircled by a crude fence made of driftwood and plastic debris. The tide was in, so the corral was filled with water almost to the top of the fence, but Brynn knew that when the tide went out, the water would be much shallower, and the turtles would probably be exposed to the sun and heat. No wonder Tully had looked so sickly.

Jade and Brynn watched all of this from their hiding place behind the breakers many yards from the beach. It was now quite dark, but they watched

Ian Fletcher as he heaved a pile of stale-looking seagrass inside the corral. The turtles swam sluggishly to the food and began to chew it sullenly. One of the big work turtles tried climbing up onto the fence as though he would escape, but Ian Fletcher kicked at him and the turtle withdrew.

"Dumb animals," muttered Ian Fletcher. "I'm not letting a single one of you out of here until your work is done." He made his way around the fence, making sure it was sturdy and held fast, and then he dove into the water and was lost from the view of the two mermaids.

"Where'd he go?" hissed Brynn.

"I don't know!" Jade answered.

They looked around, above, and beneath the water, but Ian Fletcher was gone.

"Guess he's gone back home," said Jade. "So, let's go get your turtle."

Brynn and Jade swam cautiously through the shallow water of the beach. They looked to the right and left as they neared the corral. The waves crashed on the sand and then retreated. After what felt like an eternity, they reached the corral.

They looked through the fence, searching for Tully. He was at the bottom of the corral, snoozing in a fitful, feverish sleep.

"Tully!" cried Brynn, louder than she'd intended.

Tully revived a little and looked her way. The poor turtle looked thin and exhausted, with dark circles around his eyes and a pallid complexion, but he brightened when he saw Brynn. He swam to the side of the corral and pressed his head through so that Brynn could pat his head. His stumpy tail was wagging furiously.

"This is not a well turtle," said Jade with a frown.

"He's exhausted and sick!" said Brynn. "And he's got bruises all over him. We've got to get him out!"

The mermaids helped Tully out of the corral over the top of the fence, and they prepared to get home as quickly as possible, but the little turtle could barely swim and could not keep up with them.

"If I take him home like this," said Brynn, "he'll have trouble surfacing. Jade, please, can you heal him?"

"I can try," Jade said. "But I'm still a beginner. We've only learned the most basic healing spell. It's not very powerful."

"Please try anyway," said Brynn.

Jade held both hands in front of her. A blue glow descended upon the turtle. The bruises lightened and some of the bright colors came back into Tully's shell and scales, but they could see he was not fully recovered.

"Think you can swim now, Tully?" Brynn asked.

Tully managed a kind of shrugging motion, as though he wasn't sure. Also, he kept looking at the other work turtles still milling inside the rough-hewn corral.

"I think he feels bad for the other turtles, Jade."

"Think we should release them? Can you imagine how angry your dagon friend will be then?"

"These turtles are obviously in terrible shape," Brynn reasoned. "They've been mistreated and whipped and worked to exhaustion. We're supposed to be sea guardians, aren't we? We can't leave them here."

"I'm beginning to understand how you got yourself into so much trouble, Brynn Finley," said Jade. "But I think you're right. I'd feel awful if we left these poor turtles here to be whipped and ordered around. Let's get 'em out."

"Hear that, turtles?" cried Brynn. "We're gonna get you outta here!"

The two big work turtles finned over to the side of the corral fence and strained to lift themselves up. The two mermaids grabbed one of them and tried to help him over the fence. But it hadn't been easy for them to get Tully out of the corral, and he was the smallest of the crew.

"Who knew sea turtles could be so heavy!" grunted Brynn as they pulled and tugged at the big work turtle.

"We'll never be able to lift these turtles high enough to get out," said Jade. "Let's take this fence apart."

"Great idea," said Brynn. "I'm so glad you're here to help."

"Yeah," said Jade sarcastically, "we'll probably be able to get into twice as much trouble now!"

They examined the fence, but this seemed hopeless, too. It was tightly braided with rusty wire, plastic fishing line, and discarded lines from human ships.

"My dad has a super-sharp knife for jobs like this," complained Brynn.

Jade rummaged in her purse. "How about a nail file?"

Brynn grinned. "Better than nothing, I guess."

But just as the mermaids began to saw at the fastenings of the corral with the little file, they heard a deep, unfriendly voice from behind them.

"I guess some little mermaids just never learn their lesson."

The mermaids turned around with a frantic start. It was Ian Fletcher. Coiled in his hand was the livestock whip he used to make his turtles work harder.

"It's no problem," he said, his voice dripping with menace. "I'll teach you your lessons once and for all."

CHAPTER THIRTEEN

*a*s Ian Fletcher slid through the dark water toward Brynn and Jade, he let his whip slowly unwrap itself. The mermaids fluttered their tail fins desperately, pressing their backs to the corral fence. With a cruel, toothy smile, Ian brandished the whip, and it made a loud *snap!* over their heads. Tully burrowed behind Brynn's fin and hid there, trembling.

"What are you going to do now, little mermaid," said Ian to Brynn. "Will you try another of your so-called spells?"

"No, but I might." Another voice drifted through the darkness. But this wasn't a deep voice or a menacing one. In fact, Brynn thought it was a beautiful voice, like that of some wonderful queen. It was clear and pretty like the ringing of a bell.

Ian's gaze darted from side to side, behind, and

above, to find the source of the voice. Brynn and Jade looked around, too. Even Tully poked his head out to see.

It was Phaedra. And so it was not the voice of a queen, but a witch. The sea witch. She seemed to materialize from the gloomy sea just behind and slightly above Ian Fletcher.

"Miss Phaedra," said Ian. He practically bowed down—perhaps as if he really were addressing a queen. "I-I didn't know y-you'd be here—"

"Obviously," said Phaedra.

She floated down until she hovered between Ian Fletcher and the cowering mermaids. Her pale skin shone luminously in the evening light, and her silky black hair floated elegantly in the tide. She turned to address Brynn and Jade.

"Hello, little mermaids. I hope Mr. Fletcher didn't frighten you too badly?"

Brynn and Jade clung to each other, trembling. They said nothing in reply. In reality, they weren't sure whether to be terrified or spellbound by Phaedra's presence. On the one hand, she was imposing and intimidating and she'd always been rumored to be something of an evil entity. On the other hand, everything about her was remarkably beautiful, from her perfectly black hair to her pearlescent skin to her deep-green eyes. Her long legs scissored slowly through the water as she floated above Brynn and Jade, just a few tail strokes away. Even Phaedra's voice was hypnotically pretty. It seemed to echo through the water and through their minds.

"Oh," said the sea witch. "Forgive me. I don't think we've been properly introduced. I am Phaedra. Some call me the sea witch, though I don't care for that name. And who might you be?"

"I'm, uhm, I mean, hello, my n-name is—" Brynn stuttered. "I'm Brynn."

"Yes," added Jade. "She's Brynn and I'm Jade."

Phaedra smiled down at them. "What a pretty pair of young mermaids. And who is your little friend there?"

The mermaids turned to Tully, who was practically burrowing into the seafloor, so frightened he was.

"This is my pet sea turtle, Tully," said Brynn.

"My, my," said Phaedra, her voice echoing brilliantly, "what an adorable little pal you have. Oh, but he's hurt. I can see it from here. What's happened to him? He's bruised. He's sick."

"Yeah," said Brynn. "He's been, well, he's been mistreated." As she said this, Brynn shot a glare at Ian Fletcher, who continued to bow before Phaedra, his master.

"Come to me, little turtle," said Phaedra, beckoning for Tully with her white hands. Her long and delicately webbed fingers curled and uncurled, as though pulling the turtle to her.

Tully looked at Phaedra, and then he began to

swim slowly in her direction. His eyes were lidded and sleepy, as though he were hypnotized.

"That's a good boy," Phaedra crooned, her voice low and tender. "Tully?" she asked. "Is that his name?"

Brynn and Jade nodded, their eyes wide.

"Come here, Tully," Phaedra purred. "Come here and let me heal you."

Tully floated dreamily into Phaedra's arms as if he'd been led on a wire. Phaedra placed her hand on Tully's shell, and soon Tully was enveloped in a deep violet light. Even at a distance and in the gloom, Brynn could see Tully's bruises vanish. The vibrant color came back into his leathery scales, and his eyes cleared. He seemed to grin now. Brynn could see that he was feeling much better.

"Tully," said Brynn with a little whistle. "Come back. Come on back now, boy."

The sea witch smiled and stroked Tully's flipper. Then she looked at Brynn.

Brynn patted her thigh and whistled for Tully again, but Tully held still, letting the sea witch pat his head and scratch his belly. For a moment, Brynn thought she might not get Tully back after all.

"Yes, Tully," said Phaedra at last. She opened her arms and released Tully. "Go back to your mermaid, Tully."

Tully swam back to Brynn. He looked brand new and very happy. There was no sign of any bruises, and even the faint scars that remained on his leathery armor after he'd gotten tangled in the fishing line were gone. His eyes sparkled and he nudged Brynn with his big, flat head, the way he used to when he wanted to play. Brynn wrapped an arm around his neck and watched Phaedra as she drifted down, coming closer.

Phaedra turned to Ian, who bowed even further. "Ian, let these other turtles go," she said.

"But, Phaedra," cried Ian. "Then how will I—"

The sea witch cut him off. "I have a new plan," she said. "You won't be needing them."

Ian glumly moved toward the fencing and began tearing it down. With his size and strength, he easily broke the fence apart—a task that had seemed almost impossible to the two mermaids.

"Thank you, Miss Phaedra," Brynn stammered. "How can I ever thank you?"

"Oh, that's not necessary," said Phaedra. "I'm only glad we had a chance to meet, and that I could be of some assistance to your adorable little Tully." Then she glanced around at the darkening ocean. "But it's getting fairly late, mermaids. You two should probably be getting home. Your parents will worry."

Brynn and Jade nodded.

"Very well," said Phaedra, her voice dripping with kindness. "Good night. Maybe we'll cross paths again." She turned to swim away, but then she paused and turned to face the mermaids again. "Actually, perhaps you could do me a favor."

"Us?" said Brynn. "A favor?"

"Oh, it's nothing really," Phaedra said, "but if you really did want to thank me, I could use a couple mermaids with good singing voices. Don't all mermaids have pretty voices?"

They nodded again.

"Excellent," said Phaedra. "Then meet me at the quarries on Saturday morning."

Jade shot Brynn a skeptical glance. Then she said, "Why? What for?"

"Oh, there'll be time to explain that later," said Phaedra.

"No, explain now," said Jade, folding her arms.

"Jade," Brynn hissed. "Don't be rude."

"This smells fishy, Brynn," whispered Jade. "She happens to show up just now? Then she needs a favor?"

"Listen, mermaids," said Phaedra, "if it's too much trouble, I won't impose. I'm sure you'd rather spend your Saturday playing with little Tully, now that he's feeling so much better." She grinned at Jade and Brynn. Her teeth were straight and beautifully white. They glowed eerily in the dark water.

"Brynn never asked you to heal Tully," said Jade. "Our parents or teachers could have done it just as well."

"Yes, of course, they could have," said Phaedra.

"Oooh, but then there would have been so much awkward explaining to do, don't you think?"

"No, no," said Brynn. "It's no trouble. We can sing well, and we'll be here on Saturday morning!"

"Good," said Phaedra. She pointed at Brynn and said, "Your magic is exceptionally strong. Did you know that?"

Brynn only blinked back at Phaedra. She didn't know how to answer. Was Phaedra joking?

"Yes, you have very strong potential," drawled the sea witch, as if she could feel magic radiating from Brynn. Then she regarded Jade. "Hmm, you've got potential, too. I'll need both of you to help me," added Phaedra. "That is, if it's not too much trouble."

"Yes!" Brynn cried. "We'll be here!"

THE NEXT DAY, Brynn floated to school almost without a hint of anxiety. Just about all of her problems had been solved—sort of. She'd told her mom and dad that she'd been out so late the night before because she went looking for Tully and had lost track of time—which was actually kind of true. And Adrian and Dana were so pleased to discover that Tully was safe and home again, they didn't ask any other questions, which meant Brynn didn't have to tell any additional convoluted lies. Brynn still hadn't told them what had been going on, and she felt guilty about that, but the sea witch Phaedra herself had told her that she had strong magic potential, so maybe there was hope for Brynn to learn magic on her own. After many weeks, Brynn allowed herself to hope that maybe her troubles were behind her at last.

She was sitting in her first-hour class, language arts, listening (sort of) to her teacher lecturing about the book *Land and Man: Myths and Legends* when Principal Shipley and Windy Meyers slid into the back of the classroom.

Miss Wallace stopped reading and said, "Hello, Principal. Hello, Mrs. Meyers. What can we do for you?"

"Sorry to interrupt," said Mr. Shipley. "We'd like to see Brynn Finley if we could. Right now."

Brynn's heart very nearly leaped out of her chest. This was it. She'd been caught somehow. Someone had found the talisman, or someone had seen her with Ian Fletcher. Somehow, they'd found out that she had cheated on the midterm. Brynn swallowed hard and her face colored crimson as she gathered up her class book and notebook and put them in her backpack. The class stared at her as she rose from her desk and swam slowly to the door, but she held back her tears. She'd take her punishment, and in that moment, she promised herself she'd do better in the future.

Principal Shipley was a heavy-set merman with a broad face and friendly eyes. He was a nice principal, but he looked flustered and nervous. "Ms. Finley," he said, "come with us to my office. Your parents are there. We have something to discuss."

Brynn nodded and looked at Windy. She wore a sad smile. If her parents were there, it was even worse than she thought.

Brynn stared at the ground as she followed Principal Shipley and Windy through the school. Her tail dragged behind her as she slowly swam. What were the consequences of cheating? Detention? Suspension? *Expulsion?* She'd get a score of zero on her midterm exam, and she might flunk the whole class. And if she flunked Intro to Magic, she might have to be held back. But as awful as Brynn felt about all of those things, they paled in comparison to the awful feeling of knowing her parents were about to find out she had lied and cheated. Still, she thought, it was no worse than she deserved.

Brynn's little heart was almost breaking as Principal Shipley opened the door of his office. Brynn's parents sat waiting for her. Her mother had her tail wrapped delicately around the leg of her chair, her handbag waiting in her lap. Her father sat on the edge of his seat, his shimmering blue and green tail matching the teal color of the chair. Both of them had large eyes and a look of anticipation, which told Brynn that they didn't know yet why they were there. Brynn hung her head in sadness.

Principal Shipley greeted Brynn's parents and

shook their hands. Then he motioned for Brynn and Windy Meyers to have seats in the two other chairs. Then he took a seat behind his desk.

"Mrs. Finley, Mr. Finley," he said, his voice heavy and serious, "thank you so much for joining us today. I'm sorry for holding such an urgent meeting, but both Mrs. Meyers and I felt that this couldn't wait. Windy, do you want to explain?"

Mrs. Meyers nodded and scooted forward in her chair. She smiled warmly at them, and Brynn was reminded of how she had helped her find her classroom on the first day of school. She was such a kind teacher.

"We wanted to talk to you about Brynn's midterm exam," said Mrs. Meyers.

Brynn braced herself, staring at the rainbow pattern of her scales in the bright light of the office.

"Brynn received the highest score in the history of our school," said Mrs. Meyers.

Brynn lifted her head.

"She's exceptionally gifted," Mrs. Meyers continued.

Brynn blinked, looking from face to face in the room. Was this a trick of some kind? Or did they not know? Even the proctor had noticed the talisman and asked about it. Surely, they knew.

"That's amazing," said Brynn's father with a wide grin.

"Unfortunately," said Principal Shipley, "Brynn's

magic skills far surpass what we can effectively teach in middle school."

"Is that right?" Brynn's mother asked, a look of amazement on her face.

Principal Shipley nodded. "Our testing proctor said he had never before seen a mermaid with such incredible magic skills at such a young age."

"She's so gifted," said Windy, "that she's been sitting around in class, practically bored to tears, while I've been teaching the basics to the rest of the class. I've been worried about her for weeks. Now I know why she hasn't been participating. Her magic skills are so far beyond the rest of the students, she can't stay interested. It would be like a college physics student forced to go back to second grade to learn times tables." With this, Windy turned to Brynn and said, "Sorry, Brynn. I actually thought you weren't keeping up. I'm sorry I didn't catch on quicker."

Brynn emitted a nervous, almost delirious laugh. "Oh. That's okay."

Brynn's parents took all of this in with expressions of happy astonishment.

Principal Shipley retrieved a file folder and some papers from his desk. "We're recommending moving Brynn up to an advanced-placement high school class."

Dana and Adrian gasped.

"Eh, that's just to get the ball floating," said Principal Shipley. "If Brynn excels at the high school, we'll have no choice but to place her in one of the nearby colleges to continue her studies."

In a matter of just a few minutes, Brynn had gone from feeling guilty relief to feeling sick to her gills. In fact, she looked at the faces of the adults again, wondering if her face had turned green or white or purple or maybe all three because that's how she felt.

Brynn didn't want to leave middle school. She never wanted to be too far from Jade, but worse than that—Brynn still didn't know any real magic! How could she study with high schoolers when she didn't even know beginner's magic?

Brynn raised her hand. The adults looked at her. "Uhm," she mumbled, "what if I don't want to go to high school?"

"That's understandable," said Principal Shipley. "I'm sure it seems daunting, but you'll be with merstudents who are not only your same general age, but they'll also be gifted, like you. Trust me, Ms. Finley, this is the best thing to do for someone with your abilities." He smiled proudly at Brynn's parents. "So, we just have a little paperwork to take care of, and then we should be all set to transfer to the high school."

"Today?" Brynn gulped.

"Wow, this all sounds so wonderful," said Brynn's mom, her eyes bright and happy.

"It is," said Windy. "The teachers at the high

school are great, and they'll have the curriculum to help Brynn's magic really develop. And the classes are self-guided, so Brynn can move as fast as she wants in the fields she finds most interesting or challenging."

Brynn thought of her life at the moment as a little too interesting, and she certainly did not need any additional challenges. However, practically before she could think of how to confess the whole tragedy, Brynn's mom and dad were signing the paperwork.

Adrian grinned. "I'm really proud of you, Brynn," he said.

"I can't wait to tell your grandparents," said Dana.

Brynn's eyes filled with tears. She wished with all her heart that she could be the mermaid that the adults thought she was. But how could she tell them now? While they were this proud of her?

CHAPTER FOURTEEN

*B*oth of Brynn's parents gave her big hugs and more way-to-gos and we're-so-proud-of-yous before they left the school to return to work. Then, Principal Shipley and Mrs. Meyers rode the speed-current with Brynn to the high school.

Brynn had been under the impression that the middle school was big, but it was dwarfed by the high school. And she saw mer-kids who looked just like grown-ups. As Brynn swam wide-eyed and queasy toward the front doors, Principal Shipley and Mrs. Meyers said encouraging things.

"With your talents," said Principal Shipley, "I just know that we are going to see you in the news someday for doing some great and important thing. You're going to change the world with your mer-magic, I'm sure of that."

Brynn nodded slowly but stared straight ahead,

as if swimming into the mouth of an enormous white shark.

"Yeah," said Windy, "and we'll all say she started at Crystal Waters Middle School."

"Yep, that's where all the trouble started, all right," Brynn muttered absently.

"I beg your pardon?" asked Windy.

"Oh, nothing," Brynn replied. "You know," she added, "has it ever occurred to you that maybe it's all been exaggerated? Like maybe I'm not actually that magical?"

Principal Shipley laughed. "Brynn, you are too modest. Windy, what was it that the proctor said?"

"He said, 'She has mer-magic the likes of which has never before graced our modest middle school.'"

"Right," said Mr. Shipley. "And he's been a proctor for a very, very long time. So believe me, he can recognize talent!"

Brynn swam into the huge high school just as the class bell rang. Classroom doors swung open and even more students flooded into the hallway. There were so many! And they were so tall! What would these older mer-teens say when they found out Brynn couldn't really do magic? They'd call her a mer-baby. Without realizing it, Brynn shrank back between Principal Shipley and Windy.

"Oh, don't be nervous," said the principal.

He led the trio down a hall and into a small class-room. Inside was an adult mermaid with neon green hair who Brynn assumed was the teacher. There were five students there, too. The teacher and students looked up at Brynn. They were younger than the students Brynn had seen in the hallway, but still older than she was.

"Brynn, this is Mrs. Lolly Andersea. She'll be your new teacher for all of your gifted classes here at the high school."

"Gifted? What gift?"

Mr. Shipley laughed. "That's just a term we use—gifted students. It means students who are fortunate to have extra talent or abilities or potential. It's like a gift."

"Oh," said Brynn.

"Brynn, I can't wait to see your magical talent and the spells you can do," said Mrs. Andersea. She seemed nice. Brynn probably would have liked her if they were meeting under different circumstances.

"Well, I'm feeling a bit worn out," said Brynn. This was very true.

"We understand," said Mrs. Andersea. "It's a big exciting day for you. It's natural to want to settle down a bit before you practice magic. After all, as you know, mermaids have to find their good feelings of love and peace in order to conduct spells."

"Uh, yeah, of course," said Brynn.

"How about you find your seat," said Mrs. Andersea, "and for today, you can just observe the class. I think by Monday you'll feel more comfortable sharing with the class."

Principal Shipley and Mrs. Meyers said goodbye to Brynn and to Mrs. Andersea, and then they did the last thing Brynn wanted them to do—they left.

"For class today," said Mrs. Andersea, "let's keep working on the skills you've been practicing."

The students moved to various parts of the room to cast their spells. Brynn was amazed at how good the students were. They really were gifted! Brynn watched one merboy who had orange hair with bangs that partly covered his eyes. He snapped his finger and created handfuls of light in different shades and shapes.

In another corner of the room, there was a mermaid with a pink and purple tail who raised one arm up and then spun in a circle, creating a bubble around her. The spell was called the bubble of protection, and it was one of the merfolk's most important spells. It literally created a protective bubble around the spellcaster that kept the person in the bubble protected from attacks. Each merperson could only create and manage one bubble of protection at a time, but they could either use it on themselves or direct it at someone else. Brynn's class back in middle school was supposed to begin learning the spell soon, but here was a mermaid who'd mastered it. The bubbles varied in strength depending on the magical ability of the person casting it, and so Brynn surmised that the mermaid with the pink and purple tail had loads of ability—her protection bubble was strong and beautiful, and she cast it with a certain flair of elegance.

It wasn't the first time Brynn had seen someone cast the bubble of protection spell. Adults did it all the time, sometimes casting the bubbles on their children for protection. Brynn was both impressed and disturbed by her classmates. Every spell they did only demonstrated that she was way out of her league.

Brynn was relieved when school finally let out. It was Friday, so she had the weekend to try to figure out what to do about this mess. She boarded the speed-current and had been riding for only a few minutes when she heard a familiar voice.

"Brynn!"

She turned to look—it was Jade. At last, a familiar and friendly face.

"I heard you got pulled out of class," said Jade, looking around and lowering her voice. "Are you in trouble? You know, for the talisman."

"It's worse," said Brynn. "They think I'm gifted, and they're making me go to high school to take advanced magic! Apparently, I performed better on the test than anyone had in all of the school's history!"

"Wow, cool!" said Jade.

"No, it's not cool! It's terrible!"

"Oh, right," said Jade, "because you can't really do magic."

"Exactly!" said Brynn in a loud whisper. "And I don't have the talisman anymore. Oh, how do I keep getting in more trouble?"

Someone tapped Brynn on her shoulder. She clamped her mouth shut and slowly turned to see who'd tapped her. It was William.

"Fair is fair," said Will, holding out a handful of sand dollars. "You blew us all out of the water on the midterm test. I overheard Principal Shipley say that it wasn't just the highest score in the class, it was the highest score in the school." He shook his head. "You won the bet. Here's your sand dollars."

"Will, I don't want your money," said Brynn. She tried to hand the sand dollars back to him.

Will swam backward and held up his hands. "We had a bet. You won. Fair is fair."

Then Will got off the speed-current and he became smaller in their vision as the speed-current quickly whisked them away.

"I don't suppose you still want to take me out for kelpshakes," Jade wisecracked.

"Unfortunately, that's the least of my concerns." Brynn released a heavy sigh. She let the sand dollars cascade from one hand to the other. "What am I going to do now?"

"Well, let's review," said Jade. "You've taken all of Will's allowance over a bet that you only won because you traded your pet turtle to a mean old dagon for a forbidden magic item, which you also used to cheat on your exam, which landed you in the high school's gifted magic program, for which you are utterly unqualified and unprepared for, and you've made a deal with the sea witch to get your pet turtle healed, but if your parents find out about even one of these things, you'll be grounded for the rest of your life."

"You always know just how to make me feel better, Jade."

CHAPTER FIFTEEN

On Saturday morning, after breakfast, Brynn left the house to meet Jade and then go and see Phaedra. This time, she left Tully at home.

Jade met Brynn by the speed-current stop.

"Are we really doing this?" Jade asked.

"Do we have a choice?" Brynn asked.

"I guess not. You told the sea witch you'd be there. She doesn't seem like the type who'd let you off the hook."

"What could she possibly need from us?" asked Brynn.

"I don't know, but she did mention that you really do have a lot of magical potential," said Jade.

"Yeah," moaned Brynn. "What is the deal with all these grown-ups? Can't they see I can't do a single magic trick if my life depended on it?"

"Careful what you wish for," quipped Jade.

Brynn didn't know much about the sea witch, but it was rumored among the mer-children that she could turn you into a sea slug. Brynn asked her mother about this once, and her mother said, "That's not something you need to worry about, Brynn. I'm sure she's a lovely person."

Everyone knew the sea witch had the ability to influence weather elements. Phaedra could summon huge black thunderclouds and lightning. She could conjure heavy winds that drove towering waves to the coast. The sea witch could even turn water to ice or make the sun sizzle the water until it boiled. Although the sea witch's magic was very different from the merpeople, who used love to fuel their magic, her power was nevertheless immense and mesmerizing and undeniable.

The sea witch was also known to use this powerful magic at times when she was angry or had lost her temper. It wasn't just on the surface of the water that her magic worked either. She could create powerful and destructive whirlpools and currents below that water. Brynn did not want to anger or disappoint the sea witch, but now that some time had passed since they made their agreement, Brynn had grown nervous. There had to be more to this little bargain than Phaedra was letting on. As Brynn and Jade stepped onto the speed-current to return to the quarries, Jade wore a worried expression, and Brynn suspected that Jade was probably having the same concerns that she was.

"Are we sure we want to do this?" Jade asked.

Brynn frowned. "Do you want to make the sea witch angry?"

"No," said Jade.

"Okay then," said Brynn. "We have to do this."

"Brynn," said Jade. "I just feel like maybe there are good secrets and bad secrets, you know? And this feels like a bad secret. It doesn't make me feel good inside. And when you don't feel good inside, it gets really hard to do magic, you know?"

"Yeah, I guess," said Brynn.

"So, I guess I'm just thinking that maybe we should tell someone, like our parents, and maybe they could help us. You know that the sea witch is probably up to no good. They say she doesn't believe in the merfolk oath, and that she only uses her magic to destroy things. I know you are scared of getting in trouble, but, Brynn, your parents love you, and even if you get in trouble, I know they'll always protect you."

"It's too complicated," Brynn said, flustered. "They won't understand. Listen, if you don't want to come, I understand. I'll just go on my own."

Jade's shoulders slumped. "I'm not going to let you go by yourself. You can't even do a bubble of protection spell."

"That's because I can't do any magic," said Brynn with a chuckle. "Can you do a bubble of protection?"

"A small one," said Jade. "Enough for me to fit in, but it's not super difficult to break, and it only lasts like a minute."

"That's better than nothing," said Brynn. "And it might come in handy."

When they reached the quarries, Phaedra was there waiting for them. She floated above the barren seafloor, luminous and lovely. She held in her hand a staff, probably magical, Brynn thought. But she didn't seem to be holding it. Phaedra's slender fingers were wrapped loosely around it, but it seemed to hover and move on its own with a magical animation.

Ian was also at the quarries with Phaedra. Brynn noticed that he was now wearing the talisman of Lostland. She thought back to how she'd traded Tully away for the cursed talisman, and how Ian Fletcher had treated Tully, and this made Brynn shudder.

"Ah, right on time," said Phaedra. Her black hair flowed all around her like a cloud of the blackest octopus ink. The hems and folds of her black dress likewise floated in the water around her. "Gather close around here," said Phaedra.

The mermaids moved close to where Phaedra and Ian floated over the supposedly enchanted boulder that Ian Fletcher had been trying to move with his team of work turtles.

"What are we here for?" asked Jade, sounding a little defiant.

"Oh, this will be very simple, young mermaids. You see, I must move this rock. It's not important why. It's enchanted, you see, and apparently, it was too difficult for my employee to move." Here, she shot a hard look at Ian Fletcher, who bowed his head in shame. "And so," Phaedra added, "as they say, if you want something done right, you sometimes have to do it yourself. Here's how it will work. I am going to use a spell to control the tides and currents to push against the rock. You two mermaids will sing me a high and pretty musical note, which should amplify the spell. Ian, you use the talisman. We'll amplify the magic and the stone will be swept aside."

Jade's tail swished back and forth. "That's all we have to do? Sing? Then we can go?"

"That's it," said Phaedra.

"But Ian told me the rock was enchanted and couldn't be moved with magic," said Brynn.

"Oh, what does he know?" said Phaedra. "With enough magic, any enchantment can be undone. Are you with me or not?"

Both mermaids nodded nervously.

"Very well," said Phaedra. "Let's begin."

"I have another question," said Brynn.

"What is it now," said the sea witch, growing exasperated.

"Why do you want to move the rock?"

"That's my concern," said Phaedra. "Now, can we dispense with the press conference and get on with it?"

"I have one more question," said Jade.

"Oh, for Triton's sake," snapped Phaedra. "What's your question, but make it fast, and this is the last one."

"Why did you say Brynn had special magic potential?" asked Jade.

"Well, because she does!" exclaimed Phaedra impatiently. "Just look at her! That's why I wanted her to come. Even though she obviously can't conjure a spark of magic, she is exceptionally magical. But never mind! It's time to begin!"

Jade looked at Brynn. Brynn shrugged.

"Give me a minute while I make some preparations," said Phaedra.

From within her black dress, the sea witch pulled out a bottle. She popped its cork off and began swimming around the boulder, dumping the contents over the rock.

Jade put a hand to her mouth, and behind it she said, "Brynn, why won't she tell us why she wants to move the rock?"

"I have no idea," said Brynn.

"This could be bad," said Jade.

"With my luck, it won't be good," said Brynn.

"We could still leave," said Jade. "Tell our parents. Tell the police."

It was at this moment that Brynn's conscience apparently agreed with Jade's. It was telling her to leave, but there was another part of Brynn that wondered if it might be better to stay and finish up this one area of her problems.

"Sing, mermaids!" cried Phaedra.

Brynn snapped out of her dithering. She saw the sea witch gesturing and conjuring, and she saw the sweeping force of moving water flowing over and around the giant boulder. Brynn looked over at Ian. The Lostland talisman hung from its chain around Ian's neck. The jewel glowed like a droplet of magma, and angry magical energy emanated from its facets to join Phaedra's spell.

Jade dutifully began to sing a high, sweet note, and Brynn joined in. At first, they struck a harmony that was very pleasing and obviously infused with magical properties, but when it was combined with the whooshing of Phaedra's water spell and the darkly red magic of the cursed talisman, the mermaid voices made a strange, eerie sound.

Nevertheless, Brynn felt powerful waves of mer-magic coursing through her like waves of the tide. This was mer-magic of a slightly different sort than they'd been learning in school, but Brynn began to believe that she really was magical. She could feel the power flowing from her, all around her.

Phaedra wore a feverish grin. She gestured at the mermaids and they sang a higher note. Their voices grew yet louder and stranger. The sea witch twirled the great staff above her head, and the seawater thundered around her dress and tresses, making them flutter and rush. Ian Fletcher fought to remain in place as the force of the flowing water became stronger. The mermaids held onto one another, clutching at a single strand of seaweed that grew nearby. It stretched to its breaking point. Brynn thought they'd be swept away for sure.

Phaedra's green eyes glowed with a sinister, blinding light.

"All right!" she shouted. "Let's make some magic!"

CHAPTER SIXTEEN

a green glow emanated from Phaedra's staff. She pointed it at the rock and spoke words in a language Brynn didn't recognize. The water around Brynn and Jade began rushing toward the rock. The mermaids hunkered down and gripped at their strand of seaweed, and they gripped at the ground and the smaller rocks there.

Phaedra ceased her incantation and directed her attention toward the mermaids.

"Louder," she cried deliriously, "sing louder!"

But Brynn and Jade were already singing as high and loudly as they thought they could. And they were busy holding on for dear life to any rock or handhold they could find. Both mermaids were sure they'd be swept away. But Phaedra demanded they sing louder. Brynn held an arm in front of her face to block the wind and water. Jade did the same. Then, by some magical agreement, they began to sing the song of the merfolk.

"*This is the land of the merpeople,*" they sang, their piping voices twisting and rising and growing mysteriously in the chaos.

"Louder," yelled the sea witch. She was still beautiful, but as her hair and the trailing of her dressed fluttered frantically in the flow, she was terrifying to see.

The mermaids sang on. "*We take care of all sea life, whether a fish, or a plant, or a seagull—*"

"It's working!" wailed Phaedra as the boulder began to shake. Smaller stones and boulders were now swirling through the water. Ian had been hugging a rock on the sea bottom, but it gave way in the fury of the pounding current, and Ian and the rock flew away together through the water like autumn leaves of kelp on a high tide. Brynn had no idea how the sea witch was able to hold her place in the water, but hold she did, and even as Phaedra's expression turned into a demented mask, she still managed to look elegant and queenly.

"Keep singing!" she shouted over the deafening roar.

The mermaids continued. "*This is the promise we give you, we'll guard and protect the ocean. And all its inhabitants, too. Because this is the land of the merfolk. And we will take care of you.*"

The two mermaids' voices blended in strange

harmonies that could be heard above the howling of the moving water and the clatter of swirling stones. All the while, the sea witch gestured madly, seeming to grab and harness the mystical resonating notes and redirect them into her spell.

Now the boulder was shuddering violently, as though it might crumble rather than move. Then it started to creep across the ocean floor. At first, it was only a short distance, almost not enough to notice, but then it took a great heaving lurch, leaving a shallow trench in its path. This raised clouds of dust, but they were whipped away by the moving water. What was beneath the boulder?

"Yes! Yes!" cried the sea witch. Her voice could almost not be heard now.

The boulder's momentum gained until it was actually rolling, blowing in the water like a sea sponge caught in a current. It rolled far away from them, and as it did, the force of the wind diminished.

Ian reappeared, looking disheveled and slightly frightened. He swam to the divot where the boulder once rested, and with his webbed hands, he brushed at the gravel and sand. This exposed a large metal door that was fastened with a large, heavy lock.

"So, that's why it was enchanted," Jade whispered to Brynn. "It's some kind of secret hiding place."

"Ian," Phaedra called, "open it."

The dagon gripped the great handle of the door in

both hands. The muscles of his back rippled and flexed. Then he planted his feet firmly on the seafloor and strained with his hands. He pulled with all his might, but the door only budged a little, held fast as it was by the big lock. Behind Ian, Phaedra spoke a few words in the strange magical tongue. She waved her hands at Ian, and he was infused with a dark, greenish light. With this magic, he seemed to grow, and his muscles bulged amazingly. He pulled again and the lock could not resist his strength. It broke with a dull clang and the door swung upward and open.

"This can't be good," Jade said, but there was nothing the mermaids could do now except watch.

Phaedra descended through the water until she hovered just above the dark round doorway on the bed of the ocean.

"My lovelies," Phaedra called into the hole that had been beneath the door. "Wake up, wake up! It's time to come out!"

Goosebumps of a distinctly unpleasant sort formed on Brynn's arms, and she felt a shiver run from her tailfin up to her scalp. Dust around the doorway opening floated up as something rose toward it.

Brynn held her breath.

A pair of dark faces appeared in the shadow of the doorway. Brynn squinted to see. They looked a little like seals—smooth features and big brown eyes, but one had deep blue hair and the other had a head of red hair.

Brynn knew they were not seals, however. The two came out a little farther, and when they saw Phaedra, they shrieked with delight and swam feverish circles around her. Their tail fins were dark, Brynn noticed, black and spindly like the wings of a bat.

From the clever looks on their faces, Brynn knew they were up to no good.

CHAPTER SEVENTEEN

"Selkies!" Brynn gasped.

She knew the seal-like beings who had swam up from the doorway in the seafloor were known as selkies, but she didn't know much more than that. Rumors and hearsay, mostly. Selkies were elusive and mysterious and perhaps even magical, but Brynn had also heard they were very good at causing mischief. Their appearance was half-seal and half-human. From the waist up, they looked a bit like merfolk, with arms and shoulders and faces like merfolk, although even in their faces, they resembled seals. It was also whispered that they could go on land and take on forms that were indistinguishable from humans.

Brynn and Jade had spent most of their lives in Fulgent, not venturing into areas of the ocean where such creatures lived. And so they gazed in wonder at the selkies as they swam around the sea witch.

"I've never seen a selkie up-close like this," said Brynn to Jade in a low voice.

"Brynn, I don't think these are just any old selkies," said Jade. "I think those are the Sawfield Selkie Sisters!"

Brynn felt a stone form in her stomach. Sapphire and Scarlett Sawfield, the so-called Sawfield Selkie Sisters, were infamous throughout the sea—they were *famous*, but for all the wrong reasons. They weren't well-known for being kind or generous, and not for doing good things for the sea, but quite the opposite.

"This is where they were imprisoned for sinking human ships!" hissed Jade, gesturing at the dark round doorway in the bare ocean bottom. "And we just helped the sea witch to let them swim free!"

The sisters were twins and their names matched their hair color. Scarlett's hair shone deeply red. Sapphire's locks were a deep, rich blue. Both slid through the water with their fat, black-brown tails, like seals, but they were both captivatingly beautiful, like the sea witch. As the stories went, it was their unusual beauty that made them infamous. Sapphire and Scarlett used their beauty and magic to hypnotize the human sailors and cause them to steer their boats onto rocks or into treacherous tides. It wasn't until the boats were sinking that the selkies' trance over the sailors would break, but by then, it would be too late. The humans would frantically pull on their life jackets, scramble onboard their lifeboats, and abandon their ships, wondering the whole time how it was that they had wrecked their vessels. If they managed to save themselves, none of them remembered anything they'd done while under the influence of the selkies.

Selkies did this because they hated humans. And they especially hated humans who dared to enter the seawater because selkies considered the ocean to be their territory. Brynn and Jade had heard about this, and they knew a little about why the Sawfield Selkie Sisters had been imprisoned.

Though it was a controversial matter, with merfolk with opinions on both sides, it was nevertheless illegal for intelligent sea beings to harm the humans in most of the ocean. Despite this, the Sawfield Selkie Sisters had continued sinking boats with no regard to the mer-law or any other law. They would have undoubtedly continued their cruel crimes if it hadn't been for the mer-authorities who had apprehended them. It had been a long time ago, but Brynn remembered hearing that the Sawfield Selkie Sisters had been ordered to serve twenty years in a mer-magical prison at an undisclosed location and to also participate in counseling sessions designed to teach kindness toward humans.

Brynn figured they had, in fact, stumbled onto the

undisclosed location, but she was also pretty sure Scarlett and Sapphire had yet to complete their counseling sessions because as they slithered up out of the door and began to circle Phaedra, they hissed, "S-s-s-sink ship-s-s-s! S-s-s-sink boats-s-s-s!"

"Hello, Scarlett. Hello, Sapphire," Phaedra said, smiling at the selkies as they swam around her.

"You made us help you break the Sawfield Selkie Sisters out of jail?" Jade blurted.

"Tut-tut," scoffed the sea witch. "What did they ever really do that was so bad?"

"They sank hundreds of ships!" cried Jade.

"I asked what they had done that was *bad*," said Phaedra, turning an icy glare on the mermaids. "Scarlett and Sapphire should be celebrated for what they did. Not punished, not locked away."

The two selkies slipped and wove around the sea witch and each other, their tails entwining like strands of a rope. And all the while, they hissed their eerie motto. "S-s-s-sink ship-s-s-s! S-s-s-sink boat-s-s-s!"

"If you're letting them go free," said Brynn, "not only is that illegal, you're probably planning to let them sink human ships!"

The sea witch only shrugged, as though Brynn had stated something very obvious. "That's exactly what I'm planning to do," said Phaedra. "But don't look so upset. Isn't it the duty of the merfolk to be the protectors of the ocean and the guardians of the sea? Well, isn't it?"

The mermaids nodded hesitantly.

"Well, then stop your fretting," snapped Phaedra. "We're on the same side. I am also working to protect the ocean—*from the humans*. They're the ones ruining things around here!"

Brynn had never met a human, but she was a little frightened by them. She paused and thought about what Phaedra said. Brynn remembered that they had rescued Tully from the discarded fishing gear. She recalled all the surface garbage she had found with her father that day. As a matter of fact, Brynn thought, most of the sea guardian calls were related to human trouble—collisions with boats, toxic substances making sea creatures sick, humans harming sea life for no reason. And of course, there was the seemingly endless supply of plasticky trash the humans were always dumping into the sea.

"You understand, don't you, Brynn?" said the sea witch, narrowing her eyes and folding her pale and slender arms across her chest. "You understand that these humans must be stopped!"

"Is it the garbage that has ended up in the ocean?" Brynn asked. "Is that why you're so angry?"

"It's that and a million other things. They pollute the water, crowd up the surface, spill oil and gas on us, and deplete the waters of fish with their nets and hooks! Don't you mermaids agree that we must protect the ocean?"

Jade and Brynn both nodded again.

"Then you must continue to help me! I'm the good guy here, ladies!" Phaedra cried, but she had a wicked glint in her eyes. "Come! Help me with my plans!"

Brynn and Jade traded a look. Neither seemed to know what to do.

"I've got no time to wait, little mermaids," said Phaedra. "Thank you for your help in freeing Sapphire and Scarlet, but if you can't make up your mind, we can't wait forever."

The two mermaids recoiled more.

"You make me sad," said Phaedra. "You're both obviously very magically talented, and I could have used the help." She turned to the Sawfield sisters. "Come, Sapphire and Scarlet! We've got ships to sink. You too, Ian Fletcher."

The four of them began to swim away over the barren seafloor of the quarries.

When they were out of earshot, Jade turned to Brynn.

"The Sawfield Selkie Sisters? We are in such big trouble," she said.

"Well, hold on," said Brynn. "Maybe Phaedra had a point. The humans have been harming sea life. Even Tully had been hurt. He got caught in some fishing line."

"Yeah, but what the sea witch plans to do is against the law," said Jade.

"Yeah. Well, at least our part is over," said Brynn. "We're not the ones who are going to be sinking ships." Still, Brynn worried that if a ship was sunk, she was at least partly responsible.

"Let's go home," said Jade.

"Promise you won't tell anyone, Jade," said Brynn.

"I'll keep my mouth shut for now," said Jade, "but if ships start sinking around here, I don't know if I'll be able to keep quiet for long."

That night, when Brynn's mother, Dana, was tucking her into bed, Brynn said, "Mom, if someone is doing something bad, is it okay to do something bad back to them?"

"What do you mean?" asked Dana with worry in her voice.

"I mean like the humans. Since they pollute our homes and neighborhoods, does that mean that we should try to hurt them?"

Dana sat on the edge of Brynn's bed and let Tully rest his head in her lap.

"That's not what I believe," said Dana. "Is that what you think?"

"I dunno," said Brynn. "It seems like they kind of deserve it."

"Hurting others isn't the merfolk way, Brynn. Everything we do is out of love. Our mission is to protect living beings. Even when we disagree, even when they are wrong. Sometimes we must be kind to people who maybe don't deserve it. But mer-magic is about recognizing that every being—human, fish, crab, plant, merperson—they all have value."

"But how do we get them to stop, Mom? How else can we get them to listen?"

Dana ran her hand through Brynn's hair. "It isn't easy, is it? Instead of punishing, we try to teach."

"But merfolk don't talk with humans. It's danger-ous. You told me that."

"That's right, Brynn, you must never talk to a human."

"Then how will we get them to stop?"

"I don't know, honey. I don't know." Brynn's mother shook her head sadly. "Still, when I gradu-ated high school, I took the merfolk oath to protect the living beings in the sea. I believe that includes the humans who travel on it and who live on the land around it."

"But what if they are hurting the sea life, shouldn't we make them stop?"

"Brynn, if you see someone doing something wrong, you should always try to stop them. Don't ever let someone do something you know is wrong without saying something. But that doesn't mean you can just hurt them. Your dad and I believe that you should always try to solve problems without violence, and you should only use your magic against someone if it is to protect yourself or someone else. Now, why are you asking all these questions?"

"No reason," said Brynn.

"The best thing to do is to help others, and that's what you'll be doing very soon—you're learning magic and you're doing so well. If you listen to your heart, Brynn, you'll know what to do when the time comes. Now, have sweet dreams." Dana kissed her forehead, then rose and turned out the light.

Brynn's mom gave her one last glance before turning off the lights and closing the bedroom door. Even though she was a parent, Dana still didn't have all the answers. The pollution in their neighborhood from the humans had increased significantly in the last little while, and because the merfolk didn't speak to the humans—the humans not even knowing they existed—Dana wasn't sure how the merpeople could teach them to not pollute the ocean. She just hoped that there would be humans who would try to help and who would be willing to stop others when they tried to do something harmful.

All the merpeople and other beings that lived in the sea would depend on the humans to realize the damage they were doing, and so Dana hoped that maybe somewhere there was a human mother tucking her daughter into bed and telling the girl, as she had told Brynn, to listen to her heart.

CHAPTER EIGHTEEN

ana had wished Brynn sweet dreams, but Brynn's night was filled with horrible nightmares. Brynn dreamed that the selkies were singing to the sailors on boats near Fulgent. The sea witch cackled and cheered the selkies on. On the boats, sailors and passengers stared over the railings at the selkies, mesmerized by their beautiful faces and dazed by the magical tones of their voices.

The dream continued, and the ocean was filled with boats—maybe more than a hundred—and their boats surged and plunged over the rough seas. Men, women, old, and young—none of the humans could tear their eyes from the selkies, and they apparently were utterly unaware that they were sailing directly into the jagged breakers of a dangerous coast.

Brynn kicked and whimpered in her sleep. Tully

snuggled more closely, but it didn't help Brynn in her deep nightmare slumber.

The sea witch laughed and laughed as the boats grew closer and closer to the dangerous cliffs. The humans just gazed at the selkies. If the boats crashed into the cliffs, they would break apart and sink. People would be hurt; people might be killed. The selkies continued their haunting melodies.

"Closer, closer," taunted Phaedra in a sinister hiss, beckoning the ships toward the cliffs.

Brynn dreamed that she swam out in front of the ships. She surfaced, waving her arms so that the humans on the ship might see her.

"Stop, stop!" she screamed, arms held high. "Stop! You're going to crash!"

But the people on the boats didn't even notice her. Their eyes were glazed and hazy, and the boats proceeded toward the rocky coast. Brynn swam in front of the selkies and waved her arms at the boats.

"Don't look at them!" she cried. "Don't listen! You'll get hurt!"

But it was no use. In Brynn's dream, the ships drifted over the rocks. Some of them were already breaking apart. Storm clouds were gathering, too. The wind began to blow, thunder boomed, and a driving rain lashed at the coast and the ships.

"Why should they listen to you?" cackled Phaedra over the noise. "You're no better than they are! A little mermaid who can't do magic, who traded away the pet turtle she supposedly loved! A little mermaid who cheated on her test, and who lied to her parents! You're a bad little mermaid!"

"I didn't mean to!" cried Brynn, but her voice was lost in the commotion. "Everything just got out of hand! I want to take it all back! I want to be good! I want to help!"

The sea witch ignored her pleas. She spoke to the Sawfield Selkie Sisters and then turned to point at Brynn. "Focus on her, sisters!" Phaedra shouted. "It's all her fault! She's the one who's destroying the ocean! She's a bad mermaid! A bad mermaid!"

"No!" yelled Brynn.

But the Sawfield sisters had aimed their charm and magic on Brynn, beckoning her with their fingers to swim up onto the dangerous and storm-lashed rocks. Brynn was unable to look away from them. Their beautiful eyes and captivating voices fogged her mind, and the poor mermaid was only vaguely aware that she was floating closer to the rocky cliffs, closer and closer to being crushed against the wall of rock by powerful waves.

"I didn't mean to!" Brynn yelled. "I'm sorry!"

"There are consequences to our actions," said Phaedra. "There are consequences."

Just as Brynn was about to crash upon the rocks, she woke up, gasping. All of her blankets were floating around the room, and Tully, who must have tired of her thrashing, was scratching at her door to be let out.

Brynn let Tully out and then pulled her blankets back up and climbed into bed. But she couldn't fall back to sleep. Instead, she stared wide-eyed at the ceiling.

CHAPTER NINETEEN

*A*lthough Brynn was exhausted from her nightmare sleep, she was anxious to see Jade. She asked her parents if she could go to Jade's house to play, but before they would let her go, she had to have breakfast and finish her chores. Never in her life had Brynn ever swept the sand off the porch or cleaned the dishes so quickly. Then she grabbed Tully and headed out the door.

When she got to Jade's house, Jade's mother answered the door and looked at her in surprise.

"Brynn, what's wrong?" said Jade's mom.

"Wrong? Nothing," said Brynn.

"Well, you look like you've just seen Davy Jones! Is anything wrong?"

Brynn thought about how long it would take to really answer that question.

"Oh, everything's okay. Anyway, can Jade hang out?"

Jade appeared, and the two mermaids swam to the kelp forest. It seemed so long ago since Brynn had played pretend magic at the forest before middle school had started. So much had happened since then, and she'd gotten into so much trouble.

"I wanted to talk to you about the selkies," said Brynn.

"What about them?" Jade asked.

"I don't think we should let them harm the humans," said Brynn as she watched Tully sniffing around the kelp.

"I don't know about that," said Jade. "Maybe we should stay out of it so that we don't get into more trouble. Especially *you*."

"But think about it," said Brynn. "We're mermaids—protectors of the ocean and guardians of the sea. We should do our duty."

"But this doesn't have anything to do with us."

"If you know someone is doing something wrong, you should say something." Brynn paused. "My heart is telling me that this is wrong."

As she said the words, Brynn felt a warm feeling in her heart that spread to her fingers, making a tingling sensation.

"Okay," said Jade with a shrug, "maybe you're right. But what can we do?"

"Let's see if we can talk them out of it," Brynn said.

This was very brave for two young mermaids who had seen the sea witch's magical power with their own eyes. Phaedra's rumored ability to turn merfolk into sea slugs was very much on their minds. They weren't sure exactly where to find the sea witch and the selkies, but they guessed that if their goal was to sink ships, then they would most likely be near the Sunshine Lagoon because that was where the ships of the humans were most commonly spotted.

As they rode the speed-current, both mermaids' minds raced with thoughts of what might happen when they confronted Phaedra.

Brynn's first thought was that if she tried to persuade Phaedra to leave the humans alone, Phaedra wouldn't like her. Brynn thought about this for a while and then wondered if it was necessary for everyone to like her. It wasn't pleasant to think about people who didn't like her. Then again, Brynn thought, three-shrimp salad was Brynn's very favorite meal, and there were lots of people who didn't like that. It didn't mean there was anything wrong with three-shrimp salad, it only meant that people had different tastes and preferences. If people could dislike three-shrimp salad, which Brynn found to be practically perfect, then it didn't really say anything about Brynn herself if some people didn't like her. She just wasn't their preference. So, Brynn relaxed a little, thinking that if confronting Phaedra meant that she wouldn't like her anymore, it might be okay. There were plenty of people who liked Brynn just the way she was—like her parents and Jade—and those people would want her to do what she thought was right.

Sitting in her place on the speed-current, Jade worried though that if they told the sea witch not to bother the humans that the sea witch might turn on Jade and Brynn, yelling at them, calling them names, humiliating them. Jade wouldn't want that to happen. No one liked being called names or insulted, but Jade felt especially strong about it. And so the question Jade asked herself went like this: Was she willing to risk being mistreated by Phaedra in order to protect humans, who were surface creatures Jade didn't even know. In other words, was Jade willing to put herself at risk in order to do what she thought was "the right thing"? Jade took a deep breath. It wouldn't be pleasant, but she decided that she could accept the risks if it meant they were able to keep the sea witch and selkies from crashing the ships.

Then, both Jade and Brynn had a terrifying thought at exactly the same moment.

They turned to each other and in unison cried, "What if she turns us into slugs?"

They both turned pale. And of course it wasn't just the sea witch turning them into slugs that worried them. Phaedra's magic was very powerful, and she was surrounded by others, like the Sawfield Selkie Sisters and Ian Fletcher, the dagon, who were also on Phaedra's side. Phaedra could do any number of things to actually hurt them, including telling everyone that Jade and Brynn had helped release the Sawfield sisters. The mermaids' imaginations whirled with thoughts of being hurt, embarrassed, and transformed into sea slugs. It was hard to think what the sea witch might actually do, but this unknown factor made the thought of confronting the sea witch terrifying.

"Maybe we shouldn't do this," said Jade in a small voice.

"Yeah," said Brynn. "We're outnumbered and out-powered. What difference can we really make?"

But just as they were saying these things, the sign above the speed-current showed that they had reached Sunshine Lagoon.

"Maybe they won't go through with it after all," said Brynn. "Maybe there are no ships to sink. Maybe they changed their minds."

"Yeah, they probably did," said Jade with a wave of her hand. "We can just check and see what they're doing, and once we see that they are just hanging out, not doing anything, you know, *evil*, we can get back on the speed-current and get home."

"Good idea," said Brynn.

And so the two mermaids and Tully hopped off

the speed-current at Sunshine Lagoon, a place with turquoise-tinted water and a reef of splendidly colorful life. It was a beautiful place, but the coral reef was dangerous to ships and boats—it was a jagged, rocky barrier that stood off from the coast. It was close to the surface, but difficult to see, and ships had to take care not to run aground on them. The tides in the area were known to pull and push ships in unpredictable ways, too, which could also cause shipwrecks.

The mermaids surfaced, and just as they had suspected, Phaedra was there, along with Ian, Scarlett, and Sapphire. Just like in Brynn's dream, they were sitting on a large rock that protruded from the water. The Sawfield Selkie Sisters were splashing the water with their tails, while Phaedra and Ian looked into the distance.

"There, see?" said Brynn. "Nothing is wrong at all. They're just sitting there."

But Jade's eyes widened and she pointed at something in the distance. "Brynn! Look!"

CHAPTER TWENTY

a mile or so away, a boat was approaching. The sight of the boat made both mermaids want to instantly dive into the water, dive deep, and swim away. They'd been warned to stay away from humans, and swimming away is what they did when boats approached. Neither Brynn nor Jade had ever actually encountered a human, but they were nevertheless a bit afraid of them.

In fact, after Jade pointed at the boat, she readied herself to dive back down into the water, but Brynn stopped her with a touch on the arm.

"Jade, the boat is so close," said Brynn. "If it keeps moving this way, it'll crash on the reef and break apart!"

"Maybe it's not coming this way," Jade reasoned. "Maybe it's just in the area by coincidence, and the sea witch and the selkies aren't even doing any spells."

"Yeah," said Brynn hopefully. "Maybe that's all it is. A coincidence. Yeah. Let's get home."

When Brynn said this, and as she and Jade sank beneath the waves, a sick feeling rose in Brynn's stomach and made her feel queasy. It was the same way she felt when she lied about being able to do magic and when she used the talisman to cheat on the midterm exam. Brynn was starting to think that she was feeling this way when she was making a wrong choice.

"Or maybe," said Brynn, pausing in the water, "we could just swim closer to the boat and just check on it. And then we can leave."

Jade wiped a strand of her white hair away from her face. "Okay, sure," she said. "Just a quick peek to make sure everything is all right, and then we'll leave."

So the two mermaids resurfaced and then swam toward the boat, the closest they had ever been to humans. For the first time, they saw the humans up-close. From the waist up, they looked pretty normal —their clothes wore a little odd, but they had the same hands and arms and shoulders as merfolk. It was the legs that looked so weird. It was just like Brynn had seen in books—the humans had long spindly legs that they balanced on to walk around.

Wowee, she thought with a thrill, despite how nervous she felt. *My first-ever human sighting!*

But these humans were not okay.

The boat appeared to be a small pleasure craft, a boat that went from place to place to fish and see the sights. Brynn would have expected the humans to be looking at the beautiful sea or the splashing dolphins or the lush green islands. Instead, all the humans on the boat, about forty or fifty of them, were lined up at the railing, staring. Their eyes looked spooky and their mouths hung open. Brynn followed the direction of their stare, and as she suspected, their eyes were fixed on the sea witch and the selkies.

Brynn had been afraid that she and Jade might be spotted, but the humans didn't notice the mermaids at all. As Brynn and Jade crept ever closer to the boat, they could see that the humans' eyes were glassy and glazed. They weren't talking or pointing or laughing.

It was just like in Brynn's dream—a line of humans at the boat's railing, standing still and staring, and none of them knew or cared that their boat was heading directly for a reef of jagged rocks and outcroppings.

Although Jade and Brynn were still skittish about getting so near to humans, they stood up high on their fins and waved and shouted. Jade put her fingers in her mouth and whistled loudly. Brynn hooted and hollered. Then they leaped out of the water and created big splashes. Some of the

186

splashes were big enough to soak the people standing at the boat's rail, but it was no use. They were still fairly far from the selkies, but still, the humans were transfixed. The mermaids knew that if the boat continued forward, it would wreck on the reef for sure.

"We should go get help," cried Jade. "They're completely zoned out!"

Brynn agreed. It was exactly like in the dream, and she knew that no amount of hollering or splashing would make a difference.

"You're right," answered Brynn, "but there's no time! In another few minutes, it will be too late."

"Then what?" said Jade. "What can we do?"

"We have to make the sea witch stop."

And so the mermaids dove back into the water and swam hard toward the rock outcropping where the sea witch was standing with the selkies. Brynn was trembling with fear and her heart pumped madly in her chest, but she swam forward. For the first time in a long time, she knew she was doing the right thing.

"Brynn," shouted Jade, "I can do a bubble of protection spell, but it can only be used on one of us."

"Put it on yourself," Brynn replied. "I'll be okay."

They surfaced right in front of the sea witch, putting themselves between the humans and the selkies. Again, it was the same as Brynn's dream, but this time, she'd do more than just shout and wave her hands around.

The selkies' brown eyes twinkled brightly, and as they stared at the boat, they seemed just as transfixed as the humans they had charmed. They hummed a haunting melody in a minor key that made it seem very spooky.

Brynn stood up tall in the water and swallowed hard. Jade did the same.

"Stop this!" Brynn said in a firm voice. "It isn't right to harm others, and that includes the humans."

"Get out of the way," Phaedra hissed at them. "You're spoiling the spell!" Phaedra tried to keep her eyes on the boat, but she distractedly waved a hand at the mermaids, and a twist of magical energy spun in their direction, knocking them down into the water.

"Brynn, I'm afraid!" said Jade.

They both felt that way, but Brynn looked at Jade. "There's two of us," she said. "We can stand up against them."

Brynn shot to the surface again and repeated herself. "Phaedra, stop what you're doing. It isn't right to harm others."

Phaedra laughed. "How cute. Two little mermaids that think they can stop me. And a bubble of protection on one of them? How quaint!"

This time, Phaedra pointed her staff at them, and a vicious bolt of lightning snarled out at them. The mermaids screamed and dove back just in time to avoid being zapped.

Again, they regrouped.

"Now what?" said Brynn.

"Well, maybe this is crazy," said Jade, "but Phaedra just said we were *spoiling* her spell. I think we're distracting them, spoiling the magic. Maybe if we just keep bothering them, they'll have to stop."

"Yes!" said Brynn. "But if we're gonna bother them, let's go all the way!"

"Have you got an idea?" asked Jade.

"Yeah," said Brynn. "C'mon!"

Brynn swam deeper into the water. Jade and Tully followed.

"Hey, we're going the wrong way, Brynn!" cried Jade.

"Just follow me! I've got a plan."

Once they'd swam down deep, almost to the bottom of the reef, Brynn stopped and said, "Okay, Jade. Tighten up that protection bubble. Tully and me will push you to the surface and we'll launch you at the Sawfield sisters like a cannonball."

"I feel like you should have told me the details of this plan beforehand," said Jade. "Is there a way to do this without me being a cannonball?"

"Get ready, Jade! Let's go, Tully! Push!"

And so they rocketed up through the water like a squad of Olympic dolphins. Jade concentrated on her protection bubble, and Brynn and Tully pushed hard.

When they hit the surface, Jade really did fly through the air like a cannonball. She landed on the rock outcropping, and the Sawfield Selkie Sisters scrambled back into the water. Phaedra tumbled back and dropped her staff. Jade bounced and pinballed among the rocks but was protected by her magic and eventually plopped back into the sea.

And just like that, the protection charm popped like an air bubble. The singing stopped and the magical trance vanished.

Jade pointed in the direction of the reef and cried, "Look!"

Brynn and Tully turned to see. All along the boat's railing, the humans were shaking their heads and rubbing their eyes.

The Sawfield Selkie Sisters clambered back up onto the rocky point, but Scarlett had fallen into a pile of rotting kelp, which had messed up her hair and tangled around. "Dis-s-s-gus-s-s-sting!" she hissed.

Meanwhile, Sapphire had tumbled into a tide pool, and a young octopus had taken up residence on her face. She pulled at it, but if you've ever had an octopus on your face, you'll understand how difficult it can be to get them off. "Mrfl mckl prf!" said Sapphire.

The sea witch paced around by the shore shouting, "Where's my staff? Where is my staff?" Ian

Fletcher followed in her footsteps, trying to help but instead getting in the way.

The ship began to correct its course. The pilot had evidently gone to his station and was turning the boat away from the rocks.

"Enough of this!" shrieked Phaedra. "Ian, take care of these nasty little mermaids."

Ian Fletcher dove into the water. It was then that Brynn noticed that Ian was still wearing the magic talisman of Lostland. Usually, Brynn knew, dagons didn't do magic, but the talisman would allow him to. Ian began to pursue Jade. She gave two hard flicks of her tail and easily outran the dagon, but Jade didn't know that Ian was wearing the talisman and could cast any spells. Jade looked back at Ian and was confused when he put his hands together, forming a sphere of magical energy, the same way that the mer-students did when they conducted the energy sphere spell.

"Look out, Jade!" Brynn shouted.

When Ian pulled his hands apart, there was a ball of buzzing magical power in each hand. He hurled one at Jade, and it hit her in the shoulder.

Stunned, Jade tried to move, to swim behind a great growth of coral, but Ian had already thrown the second ball, and it hit her square in the tailfin.

"Jade!" Brynn yelled. She swam frantically toward Jade as she spiraled down through the water like a stunned anchovy. Brynn swam to catch her, but

Ian laughed and put his hands together again. When he parted his hands again, he had two more spheres of wicked energy, and these looked even more powerful than the first two.

Using all of her strength, Brynn dragged Jade into the dark nooks and recesses of the coral reef.

CHAPTER TWENTY-ONE

*A*ll coral reefs are full of crevices, caves, and even tunnels. Interestingly, sea sponges are responsible for these. Sea sponges bore holes in the coral reef skeletons, which creates caves and tunnels beneath the reefs. While this seemed destructive to Brynn when she first learned about it in school, it was actually just part of the magic of balance in the sea—the sea sponges also provided nutrients to the coral and other reef-dwelling creatures. It was another example of many forms of sea life working together.

And it was into these crevices and tunnels that Brynn fled with Jade. She couldn't hide forever in the reef—surely Ian would find them soon—but it would buy Brynn a little time to check on Jade and maybe revive her. Brynn brushed Jade's cheek with her finger. Jade's eyes were closed and her breathing was shallow.

"Jade, wake up," Brynn cried, and she wished that she could somehow do a healing spell. It would have been better if she had been the one hurt because Jade at least could conjure some healing magic. Just in case something had changed, Brynn took a deep breath and tried to do a spell, but like all the other times, nothing happened. She began to cry.

"This is all my fault," Brynn said. "If I'd only asked my parents or Mrs. Meyers for help with my magic, none of this would have happened."

Brynn tried to carry Jade to safety by going deeper into the folds of the reef, but Brynn couldn't do it on her own.

"What am I going to do?" Brynn asked herself.

Above her, shadows flickered and fluttered. Ian Fletcher darted here and there, searching for the mermaids. It wouldn't be long until he found them. Brynn also saw the large shadow of the boat—it was again moving in the direction of the reef and the dangerous breakers. Phaedra and the selkies had apparently recovered themselves and were casting their charms on the ship's crew and passengers again.

There was a sudden and terrifying flash, then a loud bang just above Brynn's head. Pebbles and coral exploded around her. Brynn glanced around in a panic and saw Ian. He was moving down into the coral caves. He'd spotted her and had cast a magical bomb at Brynn and Jade. He was too big to swim down into the narrow crags where Brynn was hiding, but he could see her, and he was preparing more of the magical ammunition to flush her out. Brynn ducked just in time to avoid another explosion.

Brynn pulled Jade more deeply into the dark recesses of the coral, squeezing into a tight, skinny alcove. A few more explosions boomed above her, sending down showers of pebbles and pulverized coral. For the moment, Brynn was protected from the magic that Ian Fletcher summoned from the accursed talisman, but now she could go no farther. She was at the bottom of a deep, dark crevice, and she was reasonably protected, but there was nowhere to go from here. She was cornered, and Jade was still knocked out. It was only a matter of time before Ian Fletcher blasted his way down to her hiding place. And then what would he do?

Brynn risked taking a peek upward through the crags of the reef. She saw Ian Fletcher up there, searching here and there for a way down into the cracks and crevices. Then his eye fell on Brynn, and he grinned a wickedly toothy grin.

But then something rammed into him from behind. Something fast and strong! Brynn couldn't see clearly from where she was, but something sent Ian Fletcher tumbling through the water and out of sight. Brynn craned her neck and swam upward a little to see.

It was Tully.

Brynn rose up from the coral just in time to see Tully gliding in fast to deliver another wallop, this time to Ian's midsection. Brynn hadn't taken full notice, but Tully had grown quite a bit since she met him that day he'd been tangled up in the fishing net, and he'd packed on quite a bit of muscle during his time as a work turtle. Funny, Brynn thought, that he was now using his newly developed strength against Ian Fletcher himself. The dagon tried to summon an energy sphere to cast at Tully, but the angry sea turtle snapped around and rammed Ian again.

"That a boy, Tully!" Brynn yelled. "Keep him distracted!"

Brynn knew what she had to do. She shimmied back down to Jade to make sure she was okay. "You'll be safe here, Jade," she said. "I'm going to go do what I should have done from the very start. I'm going to get help."

As Brynn crept up through the coral crevices and into open water, Tully was battering Ian as though he were a green scaly punching bag. The sea witch and selkies were focused again on the boat and their spells. Brynn didn't have time to get all the way back to Fulgent—she couldn't even make it to the nearest speed-current stop. But then she realized she didn't need to.

All she needed was a dolphin.

Brynn dashed through the water shouting for help. She hadn't gone far when she met three dolphins swimming along the reef. They must have sensed that something was wrong, because they turned to Brynn with curious looks. One of them clicked and whistled at her.

Without magic, Brynn couldn't understand, but she hoped they could understand her.

"Please," she said. "My name is Brynn Finley. My friend Jade is hurt and there's a ship that's going to run aground on the reef at Sunshine Lagoon! Please get help! Get my parents! Get the police!"

The dolphins nodded their heads and swam away so rapidly, they almost vanished from Brynn's sight. Had they understood her? Would they really get help? And even if they did, could help get to the Lagoon in time?

Brynn swam back to the Sunshine Lagoon as quickly as she could. Ian was firing misguided energy spheres at Tully, but Tully was swerving and avoiding them as if it were some kind of game. Still, Brynn could tell Tully was getting tired. Ian fired a magical sphere, and it narrowly missed hitting Tully square in the tail.

"I'll get you!" wailed Ian, limping through the water. "You snotty little turtle! I'll get you and put you back to work!"

Brynn saw Tully and his expression seemed to ask

her, "How much longer? How much longer until we can get away?"

The boat was just above Brynn now, just moments from wrecking on the reef. What would Brynn do when that happened? How could she help then? She swam to the surface. The Sawfield Selkie Sisters were beckoning sweetly at the people on the boat. The sailors and passengers stood by helplessly as their vessel drifted closer and closer to shore. Jade was unconscious and out of commission down in the caverns below the reef. Tully was running out of steam. The dolphins had gone for help, but help could never arrive in time to save the ship. The situation was nearly hopeless.

Brynn knew there was only one thing she could do.

CHAPTER TWENTY-TWO

*B*rynn had always wanted to do magic. Even before she had tried her first spell or taken her first magic class, she had wanted to do magic. She admired all the grown-ups—her neighbors and parents—for their magical abilities. She had played pretend magic for as long as she could remember. No one could say that Brynn didn't want it badly enough. Her inability had nothing to do with her desire—in fact, Brynn suspected at times that she wanted to do magic so badly, the desire had gotten in the way somehow.

And there was more to it than merely *wishing* to do magic. She had conjured *something* that morning before the first day of middle school, out in the kelp forest. Brynn's dad had told her mom that she was "a natural." Even Phaedra the sea witch had said she recognized something special about Brynn—she told Brynn that her magic was "exceptionally strong."

Now, Brynn simply had no choice. She had to do magic. It wasn't about ability or potential or desire— it was about necessity.

Through the water there came an ear-splitting noise. It was a deafening combination of rocks breaking, metal scraping, and water roaring. The boat had struck the reef.

Brynn came to the surface. The boat was still upright, and most of the people were still standing on their legs, but the bow of the boat had crunched into the reef. The sea witch and the selkies were still busy with their magic, and just beneath the waves Tully was still staying out of the clutches of Ian Fletcher the dagon. Brynn flipped herself over and dove straight down.

After finding a sheltered place among the rocks, she quickly thought about everything she knew about magic. She'd paid attention in class. She'd taken notes. Brynn knew the technical steps of conjuring magic—she'd just never been able to actually make it work on her own. She thought about everything she knew. Her mom and dad told her it was all about love. Windy had instructed her to think about things she loved, things she was passionate about, and direct the feelings outward.

Brynn closed her eyes and took a few deep and steady breaths. This had the effect of clearing her thoughts and making her feel calm, even though there was chaos all around her. When all was quiet in her mind, Brynn thought about her parents, the two merfolk she loved most in the whole wide ocean. Her thoughts centered next on Tully and Jade—Brynn loved them, too. After that, a picture of the kelp forest and the little clearing she was so passionate about appeared in her head. And she was thinking about the other people and places she loved when something peculiar happened. Brynn felt an odd buzzing or humming sensation in her mind and in her arms and tail. What was it? It was distracting Brynn from concentrating on magic, and so she was almost ready to chase it from her mind, but then she remembered that Windy had told her that the humming feeling was *supposed* to happen. And so Brynn concentrated on the buzzy feeling, and she directed it outward. She cupped her hands as she'd been instructed, and she didn't open her eyes, but she thought that she could detect a sphere of mer-magical energy between her palms.

This time was different from all the other times she'd tried magic. All those other times, she'd maybe thought too hard about it. Or maybe she'd been concentrating on concentrating instead of actually concentrating on magic. Or something.

Who cares? thought Brynn. *It's working now, and it feels great!*

Now Brynn focused on happy memories—her

parents celebrating her birthday with crab cake and three-shrimp salad, having sleepovers with Jade, playing tag and having races with other mer-kids, and Tully curling up at the foot of her bed. Even though there was noise and danger all around her, Brynn didn't allow herself to think of any of that or anything bad. There was nothing but love in her mind.

Amazingly, all of this took only a few short moments. It may have seemed to someone else to be a very complicated and drawn-out process, but in reality, it happened very quickly. And Brynn still had not opened her eyes, but she *thought* the energy sphere that she *thought* might be there might be growing! As the love and concentration turned to the buzzing sensation, Brynn directed it outward, and the magical feelings grew stronger.

Was it strong enough to cast a spell? Maybe it was. Was it strong enough to cast a spell that would make a difference? Brynn didn't know. As a matter of fact, Brynn had no practical experience with magic. And so Brynn kept concentrating. She concentrated, focused the energy outward, and waited.

The people on the boat, which was even now colliding with the reef and the shore—Brynn thought about them. She thought about the humans. Brynn knew very little about them, but were they so different from the merpeople? Did their children have birthdays and friends and schools? Did they love their families and friends like the merpeople?

Brynn was certain they did. Now her mind shifted from focusing on her own love to the love of the people on the boat and people everywhere. Then, in her mind, Brynn heard the oath of the merfolk:

A merperson is a protector of the ocean, a guardian of the sea. Wherever living things need help, that's where we'll be.

That's when Brynn felt a surge of energy so strong, she felt like she could do anything.

Brynn opened her eyes.

There, between Brynn's small hands, was a bright and brilliant mer-magical energy sphere. And it was at her command.

CHAPTER TWENTY-THREE

*J*ust as every three-shrimp salad starts with three shrimps, every mer-magical spell starts with an energy sphere. No matter if the spell would be a bubble of protection, a healing spell, or just a spell of light, all spells came from the basic energy sphere. That's why it was the first thing young students learned, and that is why it was so important to master.

Little happy tears sprang from Brynn's eyes when she saw the energy sphere she'd conjured. It gave off a bright glow, casting sparks of mer-magic into the water. After so many weeks of being unable to do magic, after so many weeks of trouble, Brynn was amazed to find that she really could do magic and cast spells. But what did she do now?

She peeked out from her secluded place in the reef and had a look around. Tully looked like he was just about exhausted, just barely dodging the magical bombs Ian Fletcher was casting with the power of the Lostland talisman. Phaedra and her selkie friends had coaxed the humans' boat onto the reef. Jade was lying helpless somewhere deep in a cavern beneath the coral reef.

Without thinking about what she was doing, Brynn hoisted her brilliantly shining energy sphere above her head. Then, with magic coursing through every cell in her body, Brynn shouted, "Stop!"

And everything did.

This is not to say that everyone around her had simply stopped what they were doing. *Everything* stopped. Tully froze in mid-swim. Behind him, a magical pulse from Ian hovered in the water, just a half-second from striking his fin. Ian Fletcher was as still as a statue in the act of summoning more magic.

"Wowee," breathed Brynn.

The waves of the sea had stopped. The fish in the water hung there, unmoving. Brynn looked at the sea witch, at the selkies, at the boat, at the people at the boat. They were all frozen, as if time had stopped flowing.

"I don't remember Windy telling us about *this* in class," said Brynn as she looked around, almost not believing what she saw. Could this be a dream? Could this be some spell cast on her by Phaedra? She swam down into the folds of the reef, where a white-tip shark had been patrolling, probably looking for something to eat. Now the shark was holding still, not swimming forward or drifting away. Brynn put a finger into the shark's open mouth. The shark didn't even flinch. She swam over to a school of sardines. They were frozen in formation, all pointing the same way but not moving. She waved her arms at them, waved her bright tail—they didn't move. It was real. Time had stopped. Everything had stopped.

When Brynn's initial astonishment had worn off, she realized that everything bordered on disaster. Her "stop spell," which even Brynn had to admit was cast accidentally, had stopped everything just in the nick of time. But what should she do now?

Try another spell?

No, Brynn decided. She'd gotten lucky. She had cast the spell she needed to cast at that moment. Brynn was grateful for that, but she didn't know how she'd done it, and she wasn't sure if she could even conjure an energy sphere, let alone cast any other helpful spells. Also, she wasn't sure how long this spell would last. Jade had said her bubble of protection spell might last only a few minutes. In class, some of the students couldn't cast a spell for longer than just one minute. This was the very first spell that Brynn had successfully completed. How long could it really last? So she got to work right away.

First, she dashed over to Tully and moved him out of the way of Ian Fletcher's magic. Then she turned Ian Fletcher upside-down and backward, and then she removed the Lostland talisman from his neck. For a few seconds, Brynn looked down at the talisman, which she had used to cheat and trick her teacher. Brynn knew there must be magical artifacts that were good and useful, but this one was mean and accursed. She wanted nothing more to do with it. She swam among the coral reef and found a deep crevice that seemed to descend forever into darkness. She examined it, and when she'd convinced herself that it was too narrow for even her to swim down into, she hurled the talisman down into the blackness and hoped that it was lost forever.

The last thing Brynn did was check on Jade. She was safe, frozen like everything else in the small cavern where she'd been left.

After that, Brynn didn't know what to do. The little mermaid couldn't do much about the endangered boat. She swam over to where its hull was snagged on the rocks and saw that there was a gaping rip in the steel. Brynn couldn't fix it or move the ship or help the people. She wasn't much good on land, either, so she couldn't do anything about the sea witch or the selkies. Once her stop spell wore off, Brynn knew everything would just start up again.

She surveyed the scene, the scene that she had helped to create. What a mess, Brynn thought.

Just then, she saw a dolphin swimming toward the shore where the boat was on the rocks. Brynn realized with a start that it was one of the dolphins that Brynn had sent to get help. What was she doing here? Where was the help? As the dolphin passed by Brynn, it turned and emitted a burst of happy squeaks and whistles.

"Hey," said Brynn, "I thought you were going to get help!"

Then there came a voice from behind Brynn. "Help is here!"

CHAPTER TWENTY-FOUR

*B*rynn spun around and saw her parents swimming swiftly toward her. They'd later tell Brynn that the dolphins had, in fact, understood her, and that Adrian and Dana used just about every mer-magical trick in the book to get to Sunshine Lagoon to help. They had used speed spells, friendship spell enhancement, and some other magical shortcuts to get to the lagoon in record time —maybe faster than the speed-current could have carried them.

When Brynn saw her parents, she hurried over to meet them.

"Mom, Dad!" Brynn cried, diving to them. "It's a huge mess. I've caused so much trouble and I need help!"

"It's okay, Brynn," said her father. "Show us what's wrong."

A.M. LUZZADER

Brynn led the way, but when they got closer to the reef where Brynn had conjured her stop spell, her parents stopped, too. Not magically stopped, but stopped in stark amazement. Their mouths hung open, and they looked around the lagoon wide-eyed.

"What kind of magic is this?" breathed Dana. "Everything's just—"

"Stopped," said Adrian in a hushed tone.

"Brynn," said Dana, "how did this happen? Why are all the fish frozen in place? Why is the water standing still?"

Brynn shrugged. She probably should have been quite proud of herself, but under the circumstances, Brynn felt a little embarrassed. "It's my first spell," she said.

"*You* did this?" her father asked, his voice filled with awe.

Brynn nodded sheepishly.

"Wowee," said Adrian. He turned to Dana and said, "Sweetie, have you ever—"

"Seen anything like this?" said Dana. "No. I've heard about such mer-magic, but I never knew it was—"

"Possible," replied Adrian.

Brynn's parents looked at Brynn and then at each other.

"A natural, eh?" said Dana, cocking one eyebrow.

Adrian shook his head in wonder.

Dana squinted up through the water at the

hulking shadow near the reef. "Why is that boat so close to the shore?" she asked.

"Oh, it's awful!" cried Brynn. "The Sawfield Selkie Sisters were imprisoned in an undisclosed location, only the sea witch knew where they were, but even though Ian Fletcher the dagon turned Tully into a work turtle they couldn't move the stone, so the sea witch tricked me and Jade into singing for her and now Jade is unconscious under the reef and the boat is crashed!"

Brynn's parents gave her confused looks, but they seemed to grasp the basic facts of the situation.

"So, where's Jade?" asked Dana.

"Down in a cave under the reef."

"And where is the sea witch?"

"Up on the shore, but she's frozen in place by my spell, along with the selkie sisters."

"Take us to Jade," said Dana.

"This way!" said Brynn. She led her parents down to the cleft beneath the reef where she'd left Jade.

"She's okay," said Dana. "Just a little stunned it seems." She then quickly summoned a healing spell, and within a few seconds, Jade had opened her eyes, yawned, and stretched.

"What happened?" said Jade sleepily. "Oh. Hi, Mr. and Mrs. Finley."

"Hi, Jade," they replied.

"What now?" asked Brynn.

"Let's take care of the boat," said Adrian.

211

The four of them swam up to the place on the reef where the boat had run aground. Like everything else in the area, the boat was motionless. The water was motionless, too, even the water that had been pouring into the gash that the rocks had torn open in the boat's hull. Brynn's parents swam along the boat and the rocks, assessing the situation.

"What do we do first?" Adrian mused. "Fix the boat or move it out of danger?"

"I'm not sure," answered Dana. "We got a boat wrecked on the rocks, but it's magically frozen in place. This is a first for me. Why don't we push it back out into open water first?"

"Sounds good," said Adrian.

Without another word, Brynn's parents conjured up the largest magical energy spheres Brynn had ever seen. They were so large Brynn imagined several grown mermen could swim around inside each one.

"Wowee!" exclaimed Brynn as she and Jade watched.

With a series of gestures, Dana and Adrian waved their energy spheres toward the boat. The spheres crackled and sizzled as they came into contact with the steel hull, and then the spheres pressed against it, pushing the vessel back like a pair of heavy work turtles. Brynn's parents grimaced and strained with their hands held out to control their spells. Brynn could tell it required significant effort, but the boat moved. Then, with a loud scraping and clanging, the boat came free of the rocks and floated heavily backward into the safer water of the lagoon. Brynn had a peek up at the surface, and she saw that the people on board the ship remained where they had been before—standing still and dazed, staring toward shore.

"Great!" said Dana. "That boat's out of danger, but it's taken some damage, and when this spell wears off and everything starts moving again, it's going to take on more water and start sinking."

"True," said Adrian, "but we should probably find the sea witch and the selkies before Brynn's spell wears off, or they'll just charm the crew right back onto the rocks again."

Dana agreed and turned to Brynn and Jade. "Mermaids, where's the sea witch?"

"She's over there," said Brynn, pointing at the shore, "with the selkie sisters on a big rock on the beach."

"We'll deal with Phaedra and the selkies," said Dana. "Why don't you mermaids see what you can do about repairing that boat."

The mermaids looked at each other, then back at Dana.

"How do we do that?" said Brynn. "Will a healing spell work on a boat?"

"Only one way to find out," said Dana with a smile.

Jade and Brynn swam out to the open water where the boat sat motionless in the magically still water. They ran their hands along the jagged hole in the boat's metal skin.

"Do you want to cast the spell," asked Jade, "or should I?"

"Well, Jade," said Brynn, "I still don't know much about casting spells."

"But you made everything in the lagoon place stop moving," Jade replied, "including the sea witch and the selkie sisters!"

"Yeah, about that," said Brynn. "I'm not sure how I did it. It just sort of happened."

"Okay," said Jade, "I'll cast the spell."

"If I concentrate on your spell," said Brynn, "will the friendship factor help make the spell more powerful? Are we, you know, still friends?"

"Of course we are!"

Jade summoned her spell and cast it on the boat's ragged breach, Brynn concentrated on her friendship with Jade, and to the amazement of both mermaids, the metal began to fuse together. Soon, the hole was closed up.

"It worked!" they cried.

But just at that moment, they heard the sounds of shouting and the crackle and zap of magic. They dashed up to the surface to see what was happening.

The sea witch had freed herself from Brynn's magic. Brynn's parents were at the surface, locked in a battle of magic with Phaedra. They launched energy spheres and magical lightning bolts at each other. Phaedra fired magic with her staff from her place on the rocky outcropping on the beach. Brynn's parents fired back from their position by the coral reef a few hundred feet from shore.

The selkies were almost free from the effects of Brynn's spell, too. They rubbed their faces and shook their heads, as though waking from a deep sleep. Everything in the immediate area, in fact, was beginning to emerge from Brynn's stop spell. The water was flowing and cresting again, and the fish were starting to move freely.

"Phaedra!" cried Dana over the sound of the magical lightning strikes. "Stop this attack! Give yourself up!"

"Never!" Phaedra shouted in reply. "Go back to your fishy caves, you pathetic merpeople! Only I can save the sea!"

With that, Phaedra hurled a furious volley of magical lightning bolts at Brynn's parents. Dana and Adrian conjured up what appeared to be magical mirrors, using them like shields to deflect Phaedra's attacks.

"What should we do?" cried Jade. "Can we help them?"

"I'm not sure, but let's get over there!" said Brynn.

The two mermaids swam into the battle. The

Sawfield Selkie Sisters were now fully revived, and they'd joined in the fight, shooting magical missiles at Brynn's parents with selkie magic. Brynn and Jade ducked and darted through the waves and explosions until they were side by side with Dana and Adrian.

"She's really putting up a fight!" said Adrian as he ducked a vicious bolt of magic lightning.

Dana ducked behind her mirror-shield as the selkie sisters unleashed a withering volley of magic bombardment. "We can't keep this up much longer!"

Just then, a sizzling bomb of concentrated magic energy from Phaedra's staff shattered Adrian's mirror shield and knocked him back in the water. He disappeared beneath the waves with a yelp. Phaedra twirled her staff and fired more lightning. Her selkie accomplices were firing magic missiles like mad. An instant later, Dana's shield was likewise shattered, and she too sank into the surf. Brynn and Jade dove under the water as Phaedra launched more lightning from her perch on the rock outcropping.

Adrian and Dana were drifting down in the water over the reef. They were conscious but dazed and obviously exhausted by the magical battle. Brynn and Jade helped the two adults limp into a sheltered place among the coral.

"Mom! Dad! Are you okay?"

"I think so," said Adrian. "But our powers really aren't meant for lots of fighting and combat."

"Yeah," said Dana, rubbing her temples with her fingertips. "Mer-magic is much better at protecting and healing than hurting and attacking."

The water above them erupted in explosions as Phaedra and the selkie sisters fired blindly at the water.

"Mom, Dad," said Brynn, "you don't know yet, but all this is my fault. I've made some really bad choices and none of this would have happened if it weren't for me. Let me go back up and try one more time to reason with Phaedra."

Dana, Adrian, and Jade looked at her in disbelief.

"What makes you think this is all *your* fault?" asked Dana.

"It's a really long story," muttered Jade.

"If we go back up there," Adrian put in, "she'll blast us all into beach sand! Brynn, why do you think you can reason with her?"

"I don't know," said Brynn. "I just have this feeling that she's not all bad. Can I just try? Please?"

Another volley of incoming magic detonated above them. Dana and Adrian traded a look.

"If they get control of the boat again," said Dana with a frown, "the humans on board will be in great danger, not to mention the coral reef!"

"If we distract Phaedra and the selkies for just a few minutes," said Adrian, "maybe the boat can get out of range of the selkies' charms."

"Okay," agreed Dana. "Let's try it, but Brynn's

gonna need a protection bubble as thick as whale hide! Come on, everyone!"

Dana, Adrian, and Jade all joined in to cast a protection bubble around Brynn. It was indeed very thick, and it seemed invincible.

"We'll be right beneath you," said Adrian. "If Phaedra starts in again with the heavy artillery, we'll be ready to pull you out of the way, and we'll just have to high-tail it back to town to call the police."

"Or the army," said Dana.

When Phaedra and the selkies saw Brynn emerge from the water in her magnificent bubble of protection, they stopped and stared for a moment. Phaedra held her fire, and she raised her hand to signal the selkies to hold theirs. They stood still, but the selkies were ready to cast more lightning, and at the end of Phaedra's staff was a hot, sputtering sphere of angry magic.

"Don't shoot!" cried Brynn. She held up her hands.

"What do you want, little fishie?" Phaedra leveled her staff menacingly.

"Phaedra!" shouted Brynn. "Please stop! We all want to protect the sea, but we can't do it with violence! You might stop a few humans from littering, but if their boat wrecks, it will hurt the reef!"

Dana broke the surface. "Yes! Let's talk about this. I'm sure we can work together!"

"There's no need for more violence!" said Adrian, poking his head up through the water.

"Fools," hissed Phaedra in reply. "You help a tuna with a sore tailfin or you pick up a few scraps of garbage—and you think you're sea guardians. And yet, the humans are still destroying the ocean! It's time for you to stand aside and try *my* way! My magic is stronger than all of yours combined. I am the true sea guardian, and if you dare to cross me, it will be the last thing you do!"

CHAPTER TWENTY-FIVE

*P*haedra and the selkies launched a massive barrage of magical bombs and missiles and lightning directly at Brynn, but they pranged harmlessly off the heavy protection bubble. That's when two rather odd things happened.

The first odd thing happened inside Brynn's protection bubble. It was this: Brynn did not get angry at Phaedra. She had every reason to, of course. If it wasn't for the excellent bubble of protection magic from her parents and her best friend, Brynn might really have been pulverized by Phaedra and her accomplices. But instead, Brynn felt sorry for Phaedra. Her dark magic was obviously powered by anger, hatred, hostility, and probably other negative emotions. In the moment after Phaedra and the selkies fired their magic, Brynn could think only about how miserable Phaedra probably was, despite her power and beauty. Maybe, Brynn thought, Phaedra had started with only a few bad decisions and then, many years later, ended up the bad guy in a magical shootout at Sunshine Lagoon.

The sea witch spun her staff above her head.

She's so graceful, Brynn thought. *So elegant.*

Each spin of the staff made Phaedra's angry energy sphere grow in size and brightness. She knew her parents and her best friend were behind her (or, in this case, underneath her), but she wasn't sure that the protection bubble would withstand Phaedra's next attack.

"A flimsy mer-magical bubble of protection," cackled Phaedra. The staff spun and spun. "Pathetic! I'll crack it like a kraken with a clam!"

With that, Phaedra leveled the staff, releasing all its pent-up dark magic, and with a single sizzling lightning bolt, the heavy protection bubble burst and was flushed away, leaving her completely vulnerable to Phaedra's next attack.

But Brynn knew Phaedra would soon be defeated, and she knew this because of the second odd thing that occurred in that moment. It was this: she spotted two dolphins circling in the water in front of her. This struck Brynn as odd because there had been so many lightning bolts and magic explosions—why would dolphins want to be anywhere near that? But she quickly realized that these weren't just any two dolphins. One of them jumped high into the air and waggled one flipper at Brynn. Even though Brynn didn't know anything about dolphin language or customs, somehow, she knew this was the dolphin version of "thumbs-up" or "okay."

But Phaedra took no notice of any of that. As she began to spin her staff to launch another devastating magical lightning bolt, she wailed, "Who will help you now, you meddling little mermaid?"

Jade came to Brynn's side and cried, "I will! And I'll never give up!"

From somewhere behind them, there came a chorus of shouts.

"We'll help!"

"And us!"

"And we'll help! We all will!"

Brynn and Jade turned around to see.

Coursing through the water there came dozens of merfolk, maybe hundreds. It looked like half the town was swimming into Sunshine Lagoon, and probably all of the police force.

"Look!" cried Brynn, pointing at the sea.

Brynn's parents turned to see, as did Jade. They laughed and cheered. Phaedra and the selkies looked, too, but they didn't look very happy about what they saw.

Most of the approaching merfolk were wearing protection bubbles or magical shields. They were using turbo speed spells and spells for strength and courage.

"No!" shrieked Phaedra. "How? Why?"

Brynn didn't have to answer. She knew how and she knew why—it was all there in the merfolk oath. The Fulgent merfolk recited it as they swam.

We are protectors of the ocean, guardians of the sea! Wherever living things need help, that's where we'll be!

It wasn't long before Phaedra, the sea witch; Ian Fletcher, the dagon; and the Sawfield Selkie Sisters were hopelessly surrounded by merfolk of all sorts, including those big muscle-bound mermen with heavy scales and long, mossy beards.

"But I'm not the bad guy," shouted Phaedra. "It's the humans. They're polluting our ocean. We must stop them. We need to sink their ships and destroy their ports until they listen to us. Look, we are all together. Help me. Help me sink this ship!"

But the ship was disappearing over the horizon. Brynn wondered if the people on board knew how close they'd come to disaster.

The chief of police swam forward. She was tall and muscular, and she didn't seem like she was in the mood to cooperate with Phaedra at all. She swam to the base of Phaedra's rock.

"Ma'am," she shouted up at Phaedra, "you are under arrest for endangering lives, damaging the coral reef, using magic for illegal purposes, and for general misconduct, mayhem, and destruction. Come down here immediately."

Phaedra's eyes darted from face to face in the

great crowd of merfolk. "You'll all pay for this, you meddling merfolk!" she shouted. "You'll all pay for this, I promise," she hissed, but then she pointed at Brynn. "Especially you!"

"Ma'am," repeated the police chief, conjuring up a rather potent-looking energy sphere. "You're going to have to come with us. Don't make this worse than it already is."

Phaedra stiffened at this order. But before the mer-police could apprehend her, Phaedra's hand flew to a pocket in her silky black dress and retrieved a small glass vial of black liquid. In the next instant, she hurled it to the rock she stood upon, where it exploded into a swirling column of magical black squid ink vapor, which engulfed not only her but the selkie sisters and Ian Fletcher. There came gasps and cries from the assembled merfolk, and the mer-police officers surged forward, but when the cloud of ink dissipated, Phaedra and her accomplices were gone.

CHAPTER TWENTY-SIX

*A*n all-points bulletin was issued for the capture of Phaedra; the Sawfield Selkie Sisters; and Ian Fletcher, the dagon, but they were not captured.

Brynn finally confessed everything. She'd made some fairly serious mistakes, and she felt terrible for every single one. After a lengthy term of detention, lots of extra schoolwork (especially in magic studies), and some long talks with her parents and teachers, Brynn was readmitted to Crystal Waters Middle School.

With Mrs. Meyers' help, Brynn began to understand the basics of magic, and as it turned out, she was fairly good at it. She wasn't the best in the class, but she knew she didn't have to be—she only had to try her hardest.

And that she did.

Nevertheless, there were times when Mrs. Meyers saw some exceptional talent and potential in Brynn, and the teacher suspected that Brynn would one day be a very excellent sea guardian. When it was time for the final exam of the semester, Brynn nervously took the test in front of the proctor and only missed one spell—the bubble of protection. Try as she might, she just couldn't figure it out.

During their tutoring session on the day after the test, Mrs. Meyers said, "Brynn, I don't think you'll need to come in for extra help anymore. You've caught up to the rest of the class and you passed the semester final. You're really doing quite well."

"Thank you," said Brynn. "I appreciate you working with me, especially after, you know, everything."

To Brynn's surprise, she was almost sorry that all the detention and remedial school work was complete. As she was leaving, Brynn thought about everything that had happened. She realized that just because it took her longer than the other students to learn the spells, that didn't mean there was anything wrong with her. All she needed was a little more time. She only wished she had asked for help earlier.

Later that afternoon, Brynn floated over the upper edge of the Craggy Deep, ready to pay her final debt. She wasn't looking forward to it. Craggy Deep was the darkest and most mysterious undersea trench for miles around. A weirdly cool flow of water drifted up from it, creating goosebumps on Brynn's arms.

"A bet is a bet," she whispered to herself.

Behind Brynn, well back from the rim of the trench, a small crowd of middle school students had gathered. They'd heard about the bet Brynn made with William Beach, and how the bet had flipped from Brynn winning to now Will winning, and now they were eager to see if Brynn would follow through and swim to the bottom of the terrifying chasm.

"Do it!" jeered one of the students. "You lost fair and square!"

"I'm going to!" snapped Brynn, turning to the mer-kids behind her. "Just hold your seahorses!"

"Will," shouted another merboy, "tell her to dive in! You won the bet!"

In the end, of course, Will won the bet on whether Brynn would score the highest on the midterm. She'd returned William's allowance to him, and she told William that she'd swim to the bottom of Craggy Deep, even though, for some reason, William himself never insisted on it. And now William swam out from the crowd of onlooking students. He first looked sheepishly at Brynn, then at the crowd, then back again, but he said nothing.

"Go ahead, William Beach!" said Brynn. "Tell me I have to pay up. Tell me I have to swim to the bottom."

It was odd. Instead of victoriously egging Brynn

to swim to the bottom of the Craggy Deep, Will looked a little gloomy. He looked down at his tailfin and mumbled, "Well, yeah, I guess."

"No! It's not fair!" said Jade for maybe the tenth time. "It's dangerous down there, and besides, Brynn already got like a million hours of detention for using the Lostland talisman to pass the midterm!"

"No, Jade," Brynn retorted. "A bet is a bet. Will paid up when he thought I won, so I have to pay up now. Right, William?"

Will shrugged meekly.

"Chicken of the sea!" someone taunted.

"Stand back, everyone," said Brynn at last. "I'm going in."

There was a gasp from the crowd of students.

Brynn stared down into the enormous trench. It was impossible to see the bottom—the cliffs on either side seemed to descend for miles before disappearing into the yawning darkness. She'd heard all kinds of things about Craggy Deep—that there were giant squids at the bottom and even that there were ancient sea monsters down there. Her father had told her the water down very deep in the sea held less oxygen, and that merfolk could "drown" if they went too deep. Her mother told her that the extreme pressure at the bottom of Craggy Deep could be fatal!

"Never ever get too close to the Craggy Deep," Brynn's mother had told her when she was only four or five years old. "It's very dangerous."

"Okay," said Brynn, more quietly this time. "Now I'm really going."

"Don't do it, Brynn," said Jade.

"I have to!" she said, feeling as though she might cry. "A bet's a bet!"

"William Beach!" yelled Jade, turning on the merboy. "You tell her this minute that she can forget this stupid bet!"

"No," said William. By the expression on his face, it was obvious that William had just had a great idea. A smile spread across his face and he said, "No, she's right. A bet's a bet."

Jade glared furiously at him.

"But since *I* won the bet," Will continued, "*I* get to pick the way she pays me back!"

"What do you mean?" said Brynn testily. "We already decided that, remember? I have to swim to the bottom of this stupid trench and possibly drown and then get crushed by the pressure and then get eaten by a bottom-dwelling sea-monster!"

"No, no," said William. "Here's the bet. If you win, I give you my allowance."

Jade and Brynn traded a perplexed look.

"But if I win—I get to swim you home."

Jade smiled. "That sounds like a fair bet," she said.

William held out his hand for Brynn to shake, and Brynn understood. She swam away from the edge of Craggy Deep, took Will's hand, and they shook on it.

The other students, realizing no one would try swimming to the bottom of Craggy Deep, began wandering away.

"That was nice of you," said Brynn. "Why didn't you make me go through with it?"

The merboy shrugged again. "Did you really fight with Phaedra the sea witch?"

"Well," said Brynn, "yeah."

"I thought maybe you could tell me about it."

"Well, let's get going," said Brynn. "I have to hurry home. I have to pick up garbage around the neighborhood as part of my punishment."

Will swam Brynn home, and Brynn and Jade told Will about the battle with the sea witch, and how the police showed up, and how the criminals escaped. Then Will waved goodbye and turned for his house. Jade turned to go, too, but then paused.

"Want some help cleaning up the litter?" she asked.

"Oh, that would be incredible," said Brynn. "Thank you!"

"Anytime, Brynn. All you have to do is ask."

Even with Jade's help, Brynn was exhausted long before bedtime, and so she slipped into bed early. Tully curled up at the foot of her bed. Just before Brynn fell asleep, her father came in and pulled the blankets up over her shoulders.

"Hey, I nearly forgot," he said. "Your report card arrived."

Brynn's eyes were on the verge of fluttering closed for the night, but at this news, they snapped open again.

"You did all right this term!" said Adrian. "I'm proud of you, sweetie. Your mom is, too."

"Aren't you still angry about everything I did?"

"Well, your mom and I try not to be angry when you make mistakes, Brynn. Everyone makes mistakes, and if we get angry every time that happens, we'd be angry all the time. We're just glad you took responsibility for what you did."

Brynn smiled sleepily.

"You don't ever have to be on your own, you know," Adrian added. "That's why you have teachers, parents, and friends. Just let us know when you need help. And when you do, we will do everything in our power to help you."

"Sounds great," said Brynn.

"You are going to be a great mermaid," said Adrian.

"But I can't even do the bubble of protection spell," she replied with a yawn.

"Well, that is one of the harder spells. But don't focus on what you can't do, focus on what you can. There's no doubt in my mind that you are going to do amazing things. I'm just glad I get to be your dad."

Brynn slid back out of her covers to give her dad a hug.

"Thanks, Dad," she said.

Adrian turned off the lights and closed the door, and when Brynn was all alone in the dark room, she cast the energy ball of light spell, causing the whole room to glow, and then she extinguished the light again.

"Tully?" said Brynn.

The turtle raised his head.

"Just wait until you see all the magic I'm going to do!"

PLEASE LEAVE A REVIEW

Thank you for reading this book. I hope you enjoyed it! Please take a moment to review *A Mermaid in Middle Grade* on Amazon or other retail sites because this helps other readers to find the story. Thank you!

Amazon reviews can be left at this link:
    Amazon.com/review/create-review?&asin=B088QR3MPH

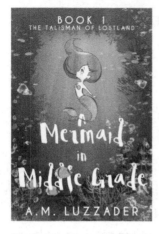
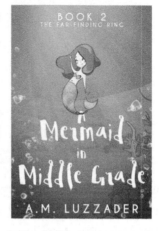
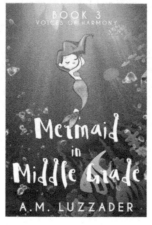

OTHER BOOKS BY
A.M. Luzzader

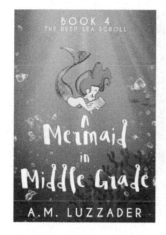

A Mermaid in Middle Grade
Books 4-6

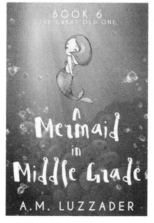

For ages
8-12

OTHER BOOKS BY
A.M. Luzzader

Hannah Saves the World
Books 1-3

For ages
8-12

ABOUT THE AUTHOR

A.M. Luzzader is an award-winning children's author who writes chapter books and middle grade books. She specializes in writing books for preteens. A.M.'s fantasy adventure series 'A Mermaid in Middle Grade' is a magical coming of age book series for ages 8-12. She is also the author of the 'Hannah Saves the World' series, which is a children's mystery adventure, also for ages 8-12.

A.M. decided she wanted to write fun stories for kids when she was still a kid herself. By the time she was in fourth grade, she was already writing short stories. In fifth grade, she bought a typewriter at a garage sale to put her words into print, and in sixth grade she added illustrations. Now that she has decided what she wants to be when she grows up, A.M. writes books for girls and boys full time. She was selected as the Writer of the Year in 2019-2020 by the League of Utah Writers.

A.M. is the mother of a 10-year-old and a 13-year-old who often inspire her stories. She lives with her husband and children in northern Utah. She is a devout cat person and avid reader.

A.M. Luzzader's books are appropriate for ages 5-12. Her chapter books are intended for kindergarten to third grade, and her middle grade books are for third grade through sixth grade. Find out more about A.M., sign up to receive her newsletter, and get special offers at her website: www.amluzzader.com.

f facebook.com/a.m.luzzader
a amazon.com/author/amluzzader

WWW.AMLUZZADER.COM

- blog
- freebies
- newsletter
- contact info